Walking

with Nessie

C. S. Clifford

First published in Great Britain 2016

ISBN: 9 780993 195723

Printed and bound in the UK

A catalogue record of this book is available from the British Library

Edited by Clive Clarke

Cover by Laura Wilde

www.csclifford.co.uk

For all the children I have taught over the years, who remain a constant inspiration to me.

And to Jo. For her formidable language skills

To Tom

Best Wishes

Prologue

Matt and James discovered a portal to another time and place at the start of their summer holidays, by chance, during their training to get fit for the approaching rugby season. While swimming underwater in the local river, Matt had found a cave at the base of a waterfall. The two boys eagerly explored the cavern and tunnel leading from it to a second waterfall. Running alongside, was a narrow ledge which allowed them to pass through the deluge into a strange new world. This is their second adventure through the waterfall and into the unknown...

Chapter 1:
Back Through the Waterfall

It had been a week since Matt and James returned from their incredible adventure with Robin Hood, and since returning the boys had been more than content to just rest, eat modern food and sleep in real beds again. They continued to spend their days together, reliving their escapades repeatedly, reveling in knowing they possessed skills different from others their age, which was great, but how could they explain the blacksmithing and thatching expertise learned in Sherwood Forest, to anyone else? It would have to remain secret to themselves, for now.

Today they sat back on the bank of the river, listening to the sounds of the waterfall cascading its eternal torrent into the pool below. As they stretched back, enjoying the warmth of the sun's heat, both experienced the anticipation of another unknown adventure, laying just a short, underwater swim away.

Matt, the younger of the two, having recently turned fourteen, leaned up on one elbow and eyed his lifelong friend speculatively.

"So, when do we go?"

"Tomorrow seems the perfect day," said James, sitting up, a wide grin spreading across his face.

"Sounds good to me! I wonder where we'll end up this time," answered Matt, with rising excitement in his voice.

"No idea, but that's what makes it interesting. We do have some sort of choice, though," said James thoughtfully.

"How d'you mean?"

"Well, when we passed through the waterfall before, we experienced three or four different landscapes in quick succession. So, we can choose our adventure by the scene, a bit like choosing an image to write about, in English."

"Except we'll be living it! I reckon we should just stick with the first landscape we find, though. It's pot luck then," reflected Matt.

"The surprise is half the fun," agreed James.

"Tomorrow, then!" He lay back, enjoying the caress of the sun on his skin again.

The following day brought another beautiful sunrise, and the boys met up after breakfast, at James' house. They fell into step with each other as they jogged towards their next adventure, their companionable silence belying the excitement and anticipation they were experiencing. James, in a buoyant mood, hummed a tune popular with the supporters of the English national rugby team at Twickenham, and Matt soon joined in.

Reaching the waterfall, they stripped to their shorts, put their clothes into plastic bags and tied the ends to keep out the water.

"Let's go!" Matt whooped and jumped into the river before his friend replied.

James shrugged his shoulders at Matt's impatience and followed. He swam down to the base of the waterfall,

6

searching for the rope that would guide him through the cave entrance and into the pitch-black tunnel beyond. He found it easily and pulled himself along and upwards until his head broke the surface of the water.

"Took your time?" Matt jibed, already out of the water and sitting on a rock beside the pool.

Ignoring him, James climbed out the pool, checking the cavern to see if anything had changed since their last visit. From where he stood, he saw the tunnel that led from the cave towards the second waterfall.

Matt picked up the torch. "Follow me, pardner!" he drawled in an American accent and set off along the smooth-walled passageway.

By torchlight, he noticed the chalk arrows that James had drawn on their previous visit to the tunnel, pointing the way home. They followed the meandering route for some distance, before emerging into a large space, semi-illuminated by diffused light passing through the second waterfall, making the walls shimmer, and giving the space a surreal glow.

"Nothing's changed since we were last here," said James, his excitement building.

"It was only a few days ago. Besides, only we know about this place," said Matt, smugly.

"I can't wait to find out who I'm going to be in our next adventure," James told him, remembering their shock at seeing their strange reflections in the pool in Sherwood Forest. "I bet we'll look and sound older again, too."

"I like how we can do things we've never actually done before. But yeah, I'm keen to learn what time period we'll be in too," replied Matt, his anticipation building.

"Well, there's only one way to find out, are you ready?" asked James, his adventurous spirit seeking fulfilment.

"Let's go for it!" said Matt grinning broadly.

They made their way forward to the edge of the cascading water and followed it sideways, through the torrent. The ledge continued beyond the falling water, until it stopped abruptly at some large, moss-covered boulders. These led them down to ground level. Matt wiped the water from his dripping hair and stared around.

"This might be anywhere," he said, taking in the view from where he stood.

"It's certainly rugged and wild, but beautiful too. That lake seems to go on forever," James replied, enjoying what he was seeing.

A vast pine forest bordered the lake, but not quite total wildness. The trees had occasional linear gaps between them, where some had been felled and obviously replanted. There were patches of natural forest, but these were separated by crop fields. To the lake side lay three tiny communities, while towards the end, at the limits of their vision, stood a ruined castle.

"Any idea where we might be?" asked Matt, curiously.

"Wherever it is, seems very isolated; tiny villages with an absence of life. Wait, there's a boat by the shore?"

James squinted against the brightness of the sun, pointing towards the edge of the water.

"You're right!

"Possibly an old trawler, which means we've not travelled back far in time." Matt sounded disappointed.

"You know, we've never considered the possibility that we might travel forward in time," said James.

"That's true, but I don't reckon so this time. Let's follow that path."

The path led towards a heavily wooded area, before disappearing into the gloom within. James fell into step with

8

Matt and the two of them followed the gentle slope down towards the trees. As they entered the forest, they noticed how densely the trees grew together, which seemed to stress their height. Thin stunted horizontal branches, devoid of foliage, punctuated the trunks up to about halfway; but from there, the branches became stouter and longer, and covered in pine needles so thick, very little light penetrated to the forest floor. Moving from day to night in a few steps, the air noticeably cooler out of the sun's reach.

They continued along the path which widened and narrowed randomly along a sinuous course, carefully stepping over countless roots that crept across the forest floor. It took a good deal of concentration and was quite tiring, both boys tripping several times before they reached a vast, freshly harrowed field.

They had hardly spoken during their clumsy trek through the forest, but were relieved to increase their pace and travel more easily on the smoother ground. James waited, as he usually did, for Matt to choose one of the two paths to follow; he had never minded Matt deciding this, and mostly, he would have chosen the same, anyway.

"What's the betting that, whichever route I choose, it will be the longest?" asked Matt, holding up his hands in confusion.

Consider that before deciding because I need a drink; the quicker we find civilisation the better," replied James, earnestly.

"This way," said Matt, making an instant decision, and setting off before James disagreed.

James smiled at the typical behaviour of his short, stocky friend, and followed patiently behind. They walked across the field, aiming for the lower end to gain an improved view of the lake. This path led down towards it, continuing along the water's edge. In contrast to the crisp, grassy odour of the field and musty aroma of the pine woods they smelt the clammy dampness of the air associated with the proximity of the lake and the sudden drop of temperature, which although only a couple of degrees, held the immediate cooling effect of placing a hand into a fridge

"This lake is massive, I still can't see the end," said James.

"If we follow this direction," pointed Matt, "we should reach one of those villages. I hope we can find somewhere to get food; I'm starving."

"Yeah, and a cold drink," James added, ruefully.

The shoreline was rocky in this area, making it hard-going, but they trudged on regardless, taking their time, until they came to a short wooden jetty reaching out into the loch. At the end sat the trawler they had seen from distance.

Matt marched down the jetty confidently, calling, "Ahoy there! Anyone aboard?" Hearing no reply, he turned back to James.

"Nobody home. I reckoned we might discover our location," he said with an air of disappointment.

As he started back to the shore, James called him back.

"Hang on a minute, Matt, see this!"

Matt spotted James' grin and stared back, comprehension dawning as he noticed the name on the side of the boat, 'Matthew James'.

"We've just found our occupation; we must be fishermen or something. Can you believe it? A boat named after us!"

Matt decided that since the boat was named after them, he could go on board and explore. James followed cautiously, and the boys took opposite ends to explore.

"Come and read this advertising board!" called Matt, suddenly.

James joined him at the other side of the deck.

"We're not fishermen," continued Matt. "We're tour guides for the lake. Only this is a lake. We're in Scotland, my friend; and this is Loch Ness, according to this, the largest freshwater loch in Scotland. Can you believe it? We're tour guides on Loch Ness and this is our boat! The board has our names, address and phone number on it too. Your name is Jim McDermott and mine is Matt Murray and, according to this, we live at Stornaway House."

"I don't suppose there are any cold drinks on board, are there?" James asked, hopefully.

"Let's go below and search, shall we?" suggested Matt, and made his way through the storm-hatch opening, turning backwards to descend the ladder there.

Below deck, they found a narrow galley kitchen and a living area, which seemed to have multiple functions. A wooden table, fixed to the floor, dominated the centre, with a bench on either side; storage cupboards were built into the walls above and below them; and two comfortable-looking, narrow bunks further on were already made up with dark blue blankets. A narrow door at the rear, with a rather stiff handle, led to a tiny washroom with shower, toilet and basin. Everything was built from a rich, glossy, chestnut-coloured wood which, although having the nicks and scratches of years of use, was attractive and cosy.

Looking at each other excitedly, James laughed and waved his hand around him. "Not much," he said, "but it's home!"

Matt laughed suddenly, as he looked at the length of the bunks.

"There are advantages to being shorter. It looks like I'm going to fit in snugly, but I don't fancy your chances.

Chapter 2:
Lorna and Lucy

James checked the galley for cold drinks but found none.

"There's coffee and tea here, and powdered milk; we could brew up a pot of coffee."

"Sounds good to me, I would drink anything right now," replied Matt, checking through the cupboards above and below the bunks.

"I imagine we must stay on this boat sometimes; there's a lot of gear for day trips, spare clothes, bedding and all kinds stowed away, but hardly enough to be living here permanently."

"Maybe it's seasonal, then. Scotland gets pretty cold in the winter, so perhaps it's only warm enough in the summer," suggested James, running water into the galley sink. "Here, Matt, check out your new identity!"

In their previous adventure in Sherwood Forest, the boys had discovered that, although they looked exactly the same as usual to each other, they appeared quite different to others, and they only saw their new personae by examining their reflections in water. They found it fascinating, viewing themselves, and each other, as completely different people.

James was already studying his new appearance with interest, when Matt joined him; he seemed to be in his early twenties with dark, wavy hair and deep brown eyes set in an oval-shaped face. Moving aside for Matt to peer into the water, he grunted, quite satisfied with his own appearance.

"Wow, get my new hair! I only hope you're as good looking as me, Matt!" he commented with a smug smile.

Matt peered into the water, turning his head from side to side viewing his own reflection. Dark hair and brown eyes, but with a rounder face. He, too, was pleased with his reflection.

"At least I haven't got a broken nose this time, he said, grinning. Looks like I can rival you for interest from the local girls!"

"They'll be a lack of people our age I suspect, judging by the size of the villages," replied James.

James finished making coffee, and the pair sat down to drink their steaming brews.

After moments, deep in thought, Matt glanced up.

"I can't imagine having an adventure here. There's a definite lack of action?" he said, forlornly.

"You're expecting too much, too soon, we've just arrived! We've already found out we own a boat, meaning we have transport. Considering the size of the loch, I reckon there's plenty of scope for adventure. Things won't happen until we meet people. I like that we're living here; it gives us the sort of freedom and privacy we didn't get in Sherwood," James replied, clearly feeling more optimistic than his friend.

"Have you ever driven a boat before?" asked Matt with a hint of sarcasm.

"I rowed one once, albeit a small one. It doesn't worry me though. If you remember, we knew how to cope in unfamiliar situations, even when we doubted it," James reminded him.

"Yeah, I s'pose so. I wonder if we've any jobs lined up at the moment? There must be a diary or job list somewhere."

"I was wondering about that too. There's a radio in the

13

wheelhouse, but I didn't spot a phone. Work comes from somewhere else, probably that address on the board. Maybe that's where we should go next?" suggested James.

"Good idea, but I'm going to finish this disgusting cup of coffee first!"

"Let's make sure we pick up some real milk later, or I'm going to drink my coffee black, this powdered stuff's foul!"

Deciding to go back on deck to sit in the afternoon sun, the boys sat quietly, contemplating the beauty and tranquility of their new world as they drank. The gentle rocking of the boat as the water lapped at its sides, combined with the sun's warmth, soon had them both dozing as they sprawled on wooden storage lockers; when an unfamiliar voice interrupted their afternoon slumber.

"Matt, Jimmy! Are you there?"

Neither responded until the call came a second time, when they rose reluctantly from their semi-prone positions, stretching and rubbing their eyes. Two identical, female figures were standing at the end of the jetty, dressed in colourful t-shirts, figure-hugging shorts and canvas shoes. Both had long, flowing blonde hair, ruffled by the afternoon breeze.

Matt did a double take and stood transfixed.

"Oh my! Are they good-looking girls or what? I must've died and gone to heaven!"

"I'm right there with you!" replied his friend, gazing wide-eyed at the unexpected apparitions. He responded to the call first.

"Hi there, girls! C-come aboard and join us!" he stammered.

They watched as the girls approached, wiggling their hips in the manner that only girls can. They crossed the short gangway to the boat's deck and walked straight over to them, planting a kiss on each of the boys' cheeks, before leaning back against the wheelhouse next to each other, arms folded in front of them.

"What brings you over here today, then?" asked Matt, recovering composure.

14

"Maggie sent us to invite you to dinner tonight. She has some bookings for you and one of them is rather special, and since when do we need a reason to meet up with you, anyway?" one of the girls asked, rather indignantly.

"You looked like women on a mission," replied Matt, a smile crinkling the corners of his mouth as he looked into her beautiful blue eyes.

"Since dinner is several hours distant, and it's a beautiful day, we thought of taking the dinghy up to Craigmire Cove and swimming in the loch. We were getting under Maggie's feet, she suggested a swim," said the second girl.

"I think that Maggie is an inspiration to us all!" James told her. "Why don't you have a seat while Matt and I find our shorts?"

The two boys descended below deck and rummaged through the cupboard drawers until finding shorts to change into.

"This looks like fun, Matt, but be careful what you say. We need to gain information from them, without giving away our situation," James whispered.

Matt was clearly on a different wavelength from his friend.

"Learning their names has to be the biggest priority!" he replied, happily.

"What about the dinghy? I don't even remember seeing one, and I've only ever rowed once before. It might even have an outboard motor and I've certainly never used one of those."

"You worry too much! Let things happen as they happen, I'm sure we'll manage just fine; we did last time," reassured Matt.

"That's true, I s'pose. We'll just have to see how it pans out." James sounded a little happier.

"Did you notice that they're not speaking with a Scottish accent?"

"Yeah, there is a trace though. They can't be from round here, at least not originally."

Returning to the deck, the girls were no longer there. Matt called out, and a voice answered from somewhere below the boat.

15

Peering overboard, James spotted the twins sitting in a small wooden craft, floating under the bow, completely hidden when they first approached the trawler.

"Guess that answers the dinghy problem," said James, rather relieved.

"I told you, just let things happen naturally and all will be revealed," murmured Matt, quietly.

They climbed down from the bow using a series of protruding wooden blocks built into the side when the boat was built. Once in, they saw an outboard motor mounted at the stern. One of the girls pulled the starter cord strongly, and the engine coughed into life.

James untied the tether to release the dinghy from the boat and pushed the craft away. The girl who had started the motor sat beside it with her hand on the tiller, but she beckoned for Matt to sit next to her and opened up the throttle, making the small craft shoot across the water at surprising speed.

They sped past one of the lochside villages, allowing Matt and James a good view of the few facilities on offer. Apart from a pub and a modest general store, the other buildings appeared to be dwellings. About forty properties were built along the narrow road bisecting the buildings.

The scenery from the boat was breathtakingly beautiful. They saw everything at close hand that they had observed from the top of the hill, except the gaps in the forest, making them seem surrounded by trees stretching as far as the eye could discern.

"I never tire of seeing the loch from this viewpoint," shouted James, trying to stimulate conversation above the noise of the little engine.

"Me neither, Lucy said she would live nowhere else in the world and, as a good identical twin, I have to agree with her!"

"What did you say, Lorna? I heard my name but didn't hear what else you said."

"I was just saying that we wouldn't live anywhere else in

the whole, wide world," repeated Lorna, turning her head towards her twin and brushing the hair from her face.

"Not in a million years!" agreed Lucy, her pride in such beautiful surroundings evident. "Can you imagine not waking close to the loch and the forest? It's unthinkable!" she said, bursting into peals of laughter at the absurdity of such an idea.

Lucy slowed the speed of the engine and headed into a tiny recess in the hillside that formed Craigmire Cove. It was a small inlet rather than cove, with a path leading up to the forest The shoreline was composed of fine pebbles offering a kinder walk underfoot than the larger stones further from the water's edge. Lucy killed the engine and tilted it upwards as the small craft bumped the bottom and stopped. Lorna grabbed the bundle of towels she had brought with her and jumped out first, closely followed by Lucy, and walked up the beach a little way where she lay out four towels alongside each other. The pair quickly stripped off their T-shirts and shorts to reveal yellow bathing suits and ran into the loch, squealing at the cold temperature of the water.

Meanwhile, Matt and James, dragged the boat further up the beach, removed their own shirts and dove into the loch, swimming strongly to catch up with the girls, now twenty metres from shore. Noisy squealing and splashing erupted from the four swimming, before leaving the water to flop on towels, panting from their efforts.

"What's Maggie cooking tonight, Lucy?" asked Matt.

"You don't really have to ask; Maggie always cooks your favourite. She spoils you two rotten. You wouldn't cope without her managing all your business and financial stuff, as well as cooking and cleaning for you, providing free lodgings in winter, *and* cooking venison stew every time you come over for dinner!" Lorna said, with affected disgust. "I don't understand what either of you did to deserve it."

"We're lucky to have her, but we'd do anything for her and, if she doesn't realise that already, I'll have to remind her tonight," said James. "Speaking of spoiled, you can't tell me she doesn't spoil the two of you as well, are you?"

"She adopted the two of us legally, which makes her ours forever. She's only adopted you two temporarily!" said Lucy, indignantly.

"It would be nice to do something for her, just to remind her we appreciate everything she does for us," continued James.

"Sounds like a great idea. Anything in mind?" asked Matt.

"Nothing yet. I'll have to think about it. Perhaps we should all work on it together, give her a real treat or something."

They spent the next hour and a half relaxing in the sun and chatting, before deciding to return to the boat. Matt and James had sought information from the girls without making it obvious. Luckily, Lucy and Lorna were happy to dominate the conversation and loved having such an attentive audience, so they had all passed a very pleasant afternoon.

After a second swim, when starting to get hungry, Matt suggested heading home and took control of the outboard, opening the throttle to speed the dinghy back. He grinned at James as he managed something new instinctively for the first time.

Chapter 3:
Maggie

Back at the 'Matthew James', the boys disappeared below deck to change and find jumpers for the walk home later that evening, on the girls' advice. Apparently, the nights were much cooler here than they imagined. Before long, they journeyed along the path to the side of the loch, arms linked with the girls, a contented spring in their steps.

Leaving the shoreline ten minutes later, they headed towards a collection of stone buildings a short distance away. The first and largest of these had a rustic-looking wooden board above the doorway, announcing, Maggie's Bed and Breakfast, short-and long-term lodgings.

The girls led inside, calling out to Maggie the second they opened the door, and head along the entrance hall to the kitchen where she frequented most.

Entering the spacious, rather old-fashioned kitchen, the girls kissed Maggie on the cheek in greeting. She smiled, giving them both a swift hug in return then looked at the boys, a wide smile melting her otherwise severe-looking appearance.

James sniffed in appreciation as the smell of the stew wafted up his nostrils, triggering a most pleasing sensation. Similar to beef but richer, more gamey; the descriptive words he sought eluded his thoughts, a small price to pay for the taste of what was coming.

"Boys! Glad ye came," she said, with a thick Scottish accent, and gave each one a kiss on the cheek and a momentary hug.

"Wouldn't miss an opportunity to sample your venison stew!" Matt told her with a warm smile.

"What makes ye think I'm cookin' venison stew?" she asked, raising her eyebrows.

"Because it's our favourite and, anyway, the smell is a bit of a give-away!" said James, with an equally broad smile.

"I hope yoo're no takin' me fur granted, noo?" Maggie's face took on a stern expression.

"Pigs might fly," Matt told her. "The girls said you're low on logs for the fire. We'd be happy to chop some for you while there's still daylight."

"Ye boys are so guid tae me! Ye chop, an' ask the girls tae bring some in, and stack the rest in the lean-to."

They went into the backyard where Maggie had received a delivery of thick pine logs. Although cut to the right length, they were too thick for the kitchen stove and the fire heating the downstairs rooms. Each log needed to be split into smaller pieces before they would be usable.

"Shouldn't take long," Matt said, selecting an axe from the pair buried in a stump used as a chopping block.

James selected the other, and they worked hard, chopping faster than the two girls could clear. The small open-sided lean-to against the kitchen wall was empty, and they wasted no time in refilling it before they cut wood for the indoor store as well.

After they had finished, they helped the girls stack the remaining logs before carrying the rest inside, as it had got dark.

"There's enough wood to last over a week, I shouldn't wonder," Lorna told Maggie. "The lean-to is completely full. You wouldn't believe how quick Matt and Jimmy are with the axe!"

Maggie beamed at the boys. "I wish others in the village worked as hard as ye two," she said, with pride in her voice.

"I bet they lack a Maggie in their lives to inspire them, like we have," said James.

"Flattery will no get ye yer dinner any quicker," she replied, quickly. "But thank ye, all the same. Get yoorselves washed noo, dinner's in aboot five minutes."

The boys washed their hands, whilst the girls laid the table and helped Maggie lift an over-sized pot to the dining table, where she ladled huge portions into rustic, earthenware bowls.

"I've made enough tae take some back tae the boat with ye, if ye like," Maggie told them and they thanked her for the consideration, already looking forward to repeat helpings the following day.

As they ate, Maggie told them she had received several phone calls during the afternoon for bed-and-breakfast rooms and for hire of the boat. In fact, she couldn't remember a time when she received so many calls.

"There's a pair of ornithologists comin' here early next week an' they requested bein' shown the most promisin' sites around the loch for bird watchin'. They're gonna be here for a week an' wud like tae hire the dinghy with one of ye to take them aboot. The girls will tend tae that, because I have a month's hire for the trawler. It appears there's a 'Nessie hunter', a chap called Ryan, comin' here with a crew of three an' they want tae map the bottom o' the loch. How they intend tae do that, they didnae say. Like as not, it's probably goin' tae be pretty borin' goin' up an' doon the loch, day in day oot, but it'll certainly pay well. It should make ye enough money to cover the winter months from this one hire. They're comin' the day after tomorrow, so ye might wanna check tae make sure everythin' is ship- shape an' ready.

"Also, two parties of fishermen comin' here fur two weeks so I'm goin' tae be really busy. I might need additional wood an' supplies an' so on, an' I'm definitely goin' tae need the girls here tae help with so many guests. It's no too bad for a day's work, is it?"

"It's amazing, Maggie, and just what we need! Thank you for all of this," Matt told her, enthusiastically.

"If you need anything, just give us a shout and we'll take care of it for you," James added.

"I've always known that I can count on the two of ye," Maggie told them, warmly. "Ye're just like the sons I always wanted, but nae had!"

Later that evening, when they reckoned it was time to be heading back, they kissed Maggie goodbye, telling her they would be spending the next day getting the boat ready for the Nessie hunters. The twins walked part way with them. They were all feeling rather dejected that they wouldn't spend much time together over the coming weeks. It was only when Lucy suggested they make definite arrangements to meet for dinner together 'at least twice a week', when things began to seem decidedly more positive.

After they parted, Matt and James discussed the evening and what they had discovered about their characters and their life.

"We're in the middle of June in 1969, so we're further back in time than I first considered," said Matt. "I saw some newspapers that Maggie uses to light the fires."

"That's good, but since we're taking a Nessie hunter around for a month, we need to research the history of Loch Ness; sightings over the years, to appear knowledgeable," replied James, thoughtfully.

"One thing's definite, we won't find a computer for research! Did they even exist back in 1969? We'll either need some books on the subject or to find somebody from round here who knows about it," suggested Matt.

"And I don't suspect there's a library in a village this small."

"Perhaps we should speak to Maggie about it. We should visit again after we've done the boat checks tomorrow. Speaking of which, what needs checking? I'm all at sea!"

Matt groaned loudly. "That's *sooooo* bad, I reckon you're losing your touch!

"We should start up the boat; we don't need to take it anywhere, just see if it works. We'll must check there's plenty of fuel in the tank and check out the radio. We must figure out how it works, at least. Apart from that, nothing to worry about. Perhaps tidy up, ensure the boat looks as good as possible. What do you reckon?"

"Sounds like a plan. This is getting interesting, Nessie hunters! And our lodgings are more comfortable," said Matt, rubbing his hands together in excitement.

The following morning, the boys woke early well-rested after their night in the narrow bunks. Looking around the living quarters in the cold morning light, they decided that the compact space would appear much better with a 'spring clean', and set to it with dusters and soapy water.

"That wasn't actually as bad as I thought," remarked Matt, when they had finished. "Just don't tell my mum, she'd never let me hear the last of it. I'd probably have to tidy my room!"

"Your secret's safe with me, Matt. You were brilliant with that bucket, so mop the deck while I attend the important stuff, like fixing coffee."

He took the mop that James held out to him but handed him a bottle in exchange.

"No problem! But you can use the *Windolene* I found in the under-sink cupboard. All that glass round the wheelhouse is looking very grubby!"

Without the fishing equipment, affixed to the boat in its previous life, the deck was spacious, but Matt still finished his mopping before James reappeared from the wheelhouse. He wandered in to see his friend applying the pink, opaque liquid to the final window, and turned to examine the covered space.

Sufficient room for four people in heavy weather, and had a sliding door to the deck, keeping it relatively water-tight. The controls were all in front of the ship's wheel, whilst the sides were shelved for charts and electrical equipment. Matt recognised the radio and thought he spotted a depth sounder that would give the distance to the bottom of the loch. In one corner, next to the sliding door, a table for spreading out charts, and a fixed bench.

He looked at the instrument panel, which didn't appear too complicated. "It looks like there are gauges for speed, oil pressure, temperature and fuel, as well as a compass and, most importantly, key ignition. It's not that different from a car, really. Let's start her up, shall we?" he said, with a gleam in his eye.

James nodded, so Matt turned the key and the diesel engine coughed into life.

"Where's the accelerator?" Matt asked suddenly, as the thought occurred to him.

"Over here, this lever." James pushed it forward and listened to the increased pitch of the engine.

"This one must be the gear lever; it looks like two forward gears and one reverse, but I won't try them at the moment." James said, before pressing a small button. The engine spluttered and died.

"Fuel gauge showed full and the oil pressure needle moved to halfway; that's as far as it goes on my dad's car. I reckon this baby is ready to go," Matt told James with satisfaction.

"Great! Then it's time to ask Maggie about Nessie," said James, taking the lead for once.

"Good idea. By the time we arrive, it'll be lunch time and there's an excellent chance for another portion of stew," said Matt, hopefully.

James laughed. "Nothing but food, eh?"

"I can't help being hungry. We've been at it for hours!

"What d'you know about Nessie?" he asked as they followed the path to Maggie's.

"Nothing really," said James. "Some famous photos taken in the past that *appear* real, and loads of reported sightings. Not a lot else. How about you?"

"The same, I s'pose. I wonder what the locals believe." Matt pursed his lips.

"I reckon that tourism is the main source of employment round here, and that's imperative for a small community. Maybe the locals pretend to believe the myth to encourage the tourists. I bet there aren't many true believers on the quiet, though."

"Well, I'm sure that you and I can become believers right now, if it'd help! But our purpose remains a mystery, and when the adventure might start," continued Matt.

"Oh, I reckon something's going to happen alright. It will differ greatly from our previous one!" said James with a wry smile.

Chapter 4:
Behind the Legend of Nessie

Maggie was bent over, pushing a mop furiously backwards and forwards across the quarry tiles in the kitchen.

"Hi, Maggie!" chorused the boys.

She straightened, ceased her mopping, and wiped her brow with her apron.

"Are you in training for a mopping competition?" Matt asked, before she responded to their greeting.

"I'll nae have any of yer cheek, or I'll be using the mop on ye, young man," she admonished.

Matt feigned a look of fear.

"What brings ye boys here today?" she asked, smiling in her usual welcoming way. "I thought ye'd be busy on yer boat, gettin' it ready an' the like."

"We've done all that already, but it occurred to us we might gen up on some 'Nessie' history to prepare for this Ryan chap. He'd expect us to know all about it and, to be perfectly honest we don't. So, we were wondering if you can suggest somebody we might talk to," said James, getting straight to the point of their visit.

"I dinnae need tae suggest anybody else, as I've kept a scrapbook of all the sightin's here since I were a wee lassie back in the thirties. I can probably tell ye everythin' ye'll need tae get by.

"Why don't ye put the kettle on for a wee cup o' tea, and I'll bring doon ma cuttin's," she suggested, untying her apron as she spoke.

"That sounds fair," replied Matt, reaching for the kettle.

Maggie returned before he had finished spooning tea into the teapot and placed two over-filled scrapbooks on the kitchen table.

"You were'nt joking about keeping records! You've recorded everything that's happened on the loch," said James in amazement.

"I have records of everythin' since 1933 when I first started the scrapbook," Maggie told them proudly.

"What made you keep them?" asked Matt.

Maggie's eyes held a faraway stare briefly, as she explained that she and a friend had witnessed an event on the loch that she couldn't explain.

"You saw it, didn't you? You actually saw the monster!" said James, almost shouting in excitement.

"I saw *somethin'*. But tae this day, I cannae say fur sure what it was."

"Tell us, Maggie. What happened?"

"There's more interestin' stuff in the scrapbooks that will fulfil yer needs," she replied, reaching towards the older-looking book. Brittle, yellowing Sellotape protruded from the edges of the pages where newspaper clippings had been stuck in, as she opened the plain, green front cover.

"Maggie, we'd like to listen to *your* story. There's no person on the planet we trust more than you, and if you're

27

worried about us talking to others, I promise you we would never betray your trust," said Matt, gently.

"Can we listen too?" Lorna's voice broke the short silence after Matt's request.

They turned to see the twins standing at the doorway. Entering, they sat down next to the boys.

"We really would like to hear about your sighting," Lorna
repeated.

"So long ago now. I'm not sure that I can even remember," said Maggie, wearily. They all waited with baited breath until Maggie finally conceded.

"Alright then, but ye must ne'er reveal what I'm about to tell ye. I swore I would'nae tell anyone, and I haven't," she said, sadly. "Not for thirty-six years.

"I was fourteen in 1933, an' like you four I was workin' hard an' enjoyin' a simple existence. I didnae have much free time, ye didnae in those days. But when I did, I used tae meet up with three close friends o' mine an' go off in the boat, rowin' aroun' the loch. They've all left the loch since; one tae study at the university in Edinburgh, an' the others when their husbands found work away from Inverness, but we all vowed that we would ne'er reveal what we saw tae anybody we didnae trust implicitly. Ye might ask why such a promise was necessary, but we didnae want the sort of publicity the Nessie-spotters usually received, an' we could'nae bear the thought of being ridiculed. To date, oor secret has remained secure, an' I want tae keep it so.

"You can trust us Maggie, nobody here will ridicule you, for sure."

"Well, one Sunday afternoon, we went up tae Craigmire Cove. It's quite private, an' has the nicest beach, an' we wanted tae swim and enjoy the summer sunshine.

Such a beautiful day, so hot, an' ye could hear nothin' but birdsong an' splashes as fish jumped aboot in the loch. We'd been relaxin' for aboot an hour when we decided tae go swimmin', an' we were happy enough doin' handstands in the shallows an' splashing aroun' in the watter, when suddenly Susan, ma best friend, started tae scream. We swam over tae her, but she was quite hysterical, saying that somethin' had tugged on her leg an' tried tae pull her doon underwatter. We helped her get tae shore an', sure enough, we saw the imprint o' teeth right doon her calf. The skin had hardly been broken so she wasnae really hurt, but she was shakin' with fright. It took us ages tae calm her doon."

The four teenagers listened with wide eyes as, barely pausing for breath, Maggie continued with a torrent of words, finally released from the silence she had maintained for so long.

"1933 was a big year fur Nessie; many sightin's, an' we were just realisin' how big Nessie was becomin'. Of course, Susan started tae say she had been attacked by Nessie an' the teeth marks seemed tae suggest that at least somethin' had bitten her leg, but the fact that the skin had barely been broken told a different story. I didnae believe she was really attacked. Almost as if somethin' were *investigatin'* her. The marks on her leg stretched doon the entire length of her calf, indicatin' quite a big mooth, an' a mooth that size could easily have bitten harder an' caused real damage. That's just ma belief though."

She paused, taking a sip of tea before continuing. Her audience waited expectantly, hardly daring to move, in case they broke the spell she'd cast over them.

"Took a long time tae talk Susan into staying at Craigmire Cove. She wanted tae return home, but truthfully, we were scared about getting' back in the boat. An' then, as we were sittin' on the shore, talkin' aboot what we would do, our boat suddenly tipped right up oot o'the watter. There was nae reason for it; was nae a bit o' wind, the loch was like a mill pond. Then it happened again. It was only a small wooden boat, built by one o' the men in the village fur rowin' aroun' the loch, but it was heavy an' would have taken a great deal o' power tae lift it; power that originated under the watter.

"As we watched, a large, dark hump broke the surface an' glided along the shoreline in front o' us. We had nae idea what it were, an' that made frightenin'. After aboot fifty yards, it turned roond an' came back again. The creature swam up an' doon in front o' us again before she turned an' swam towards the middle of the loch, an' when she was aboot a hundred yards away, she disappeared under the watter an' I didnae see her again fur nearly twenty years.

"We all agreed tae tell nobody, until now."

"Why do you call it 'she'? asked James, curiously.

"Hang on, Jimmy," Lucy interjected, "you said you didn't see it again for nearly twenty years, Maggie. There's more?" she asked, gently.

"Aye, but little tae tell, really. I was oot walkin' one day in 1952, when I saw the same creature, swimmin' along that same stretch o' watter with her great hump clearly showin' above the water. I saw her again, a few years past, the summer of '65. Again, the same place, but she had company, a wee one, her babby perhaps. I don't believe in monsters, but I have nae doubt *somethin'* lives in the loch, an' I'm no' the only one aroun' to believe that.

"There's an explanation for the existence of a large watter creature, an' perhaps, the truth will be discovered. Now, despite the myths an' legends surrounding this creature flourish an' keep us employed, nobody will ever convince me that Nessie disnae exist."

"Wow, that's some story Maggie! Thank you for trusting us," Lorna said, planting a kiss on her cheek.

"If I cannae trust ye four, then I'll ne'er find anybody I can," said Maggie, reaching for the scrapbook again. "Let's read through the reported sightin's, because this is what ye can use with oor guests.

"There have been sightin's recorded in the sixth century, but 1933 is when it all started in recent times, and when I started ma scrapbooks. So, we'll concentrate on the last thirty-five years," Maggie stated, opening up the first book.

Inside were black and white newspaper photographs and reports, with handwritten notes that Maggie had added alongside them. It really was a complete history.

"You should turn all this into a book, if you ever hit hard times, Maggie," James told her, amazed at the details. Maggie just smiled and pointed to the first report.

"July 22nd 1933, George Spicer and his wife viewed the creature crossin' the road when they were travellin' in their car. It was the first of several reports of land sightin's. The same year in August, Arthur Grant nearly hit the creature with his motorbike as it crossed the road.

"In 1934, surgeon Kenneth Wilson took the most famous photograph of Nessie, the one with the long neck.

Published in the *Daily Mail,* it has yet tae be revealed a fake.

"Next, 1943, C. B. Farrel spotted Nessie and suggested that its overall length was at least twenty-five feet.

"1954, a fishin' boat called the Rival 111 contacted a large underwatter object, just below the surface, that followed their boat fur over a mile.

"And in 1960, Peter O'Connor spotted two separate, parallel wakes movin' up the loch, which suggests two

31

creatures, rather like I witnessed myself.

"After that, sporadic land sightin's until 1962 when a group of Nessie enthusiasts started up the Loch Ness Phenomena Investigation Bureau. The locals changed that a wee bit callin' it The Loch Ness Phenomena Bureau of Investigation (known as the Lochal PhBI, the local FBI, get it?) Their members film the loch from various points around it an' three years ago they placed a caravan at Achnahannet an' built a main observation platform."

"I remember them doing that; was in all the local papers," interrupted Lucy. "They're still operating from there, now."

"That's right, bairn. Last year, the loch was searched by a special type of device, somethin' called sonar that went from one side o' the loch tae the other. A new modified system, still experimental in fact, designed by some researchers at Birmingham University. Durin' their recordin's, the sonar picked up multiple objects aboot twenty-foot in length, swimmin' at mid-watter depth. They could'nae prove what they were, but they said air-breathin' creatures could be ruled oot as they never surfaced. They ruled oot fish too, because o' the high speed the creatures rose an' fell from the depths.

"Other observations an' reports of sightin's exist, but none prove, or disprove, the existence of the creature. Some crypto-zoologists suggest the creature is related to a plesiosaur from the dinosaur age. In fact, most descriptions, appearing from the most reliable sources seem to suggest it. I know there's *somethin'* oot there but, although the practical side o' me says we need the business it brings, part of me wishes people would just let it be.

"There is more, if you wish tae scan the file further, but there's a limit tae what you would remember, anyway.

Everythin' in here is factual, and records exist elsewhere. Does that tell ye everythin' ye need to know boys?"

"I think you've more than covered it, Maggie! I suggest you keep these scrapbooks somewhere very safe. The history you have recorded here would be a goldmine to somebody like Ryan. Thanks for sharing this. I had no idea that you were such an authority on the subject, let alone a true believer," James told her, gratefully.

Maggie left them, going off to tend to her duties followed by the girls, leaving the boys alone with their thoughts.

Chapter 5:
John Ryan

The boys considered Maggie's revelations late into the night, unable to sway their doubts and accept what Maggie believed. The contrast between their own modern upbringing, where Nessie was considered imagination, and current technology cast reasonable doubt on the validity of the photographs. It wasn't that they didn't believe Maggie, they *couldn't* believe her. They both agreed to attempt being open-minded and appear to support the myth when with Ryan's team.

Both wondered what Ryan was like, and whether his reputation for being ruthless when carrying out his investigations was justified. Again, they agreed to be open-minded and wouldn't judge him before meeting him. Sleep didn't come easily to them that night, as they lay there with their minds so troubled.

They rose early the next day, despite knowing that the party of Nessie-hunters would not arrive until the afternoon. Matt suggested visiting Maggie's and offering a helping hand with her preparations, but James considered their presence might hamper them. Instead, they decided to walk into the village to explore and buy fresh milk. He also suggested buying extra food and drink supplies to keep on board, the days would be long, travelling up and down the loch taking sonar readings. Matt agreed to the idea, but expected Maggie to take cater for each individual day, ensuring their guests received the provisions they preferred. A walk to the village was relaxing though, and they followed the path that also led towards Maggie's.

"Perhaps we should call in to see if she needs anything as we're passing," suggested Matt.

"Is it Maggie you want to see or the twins?" teased James.

"Well, I wouldn't mind spending more time with the girls, but I expect they'll be busy helping Maggie. No, my real reason is simply repaying the kindness she always shows us."

"I know what you mean. It won't hurt to pop in as we pass," said James.

The Bed-and-Breakfast was buzzing with activity, and with nothing required from the village, the boys journeyed onwards, unwilling to distract the women from their preparations. After a brief period exploring the village and conversing with the locals, they head back, wondering how to spend their free time.

During the middle of the afternoon, Lucy and Lorna came down to fetch the boys after John Ryan's arrival. He had specifically requested meeting them, wanting to explore the details of his expected achievements.

By then, they were bored with their own company, and were pleased with the twin's arrival, wasting no time in returning to Maggie's. Perhaps, finally, their adventure would begin!

Lucy led them to the large seating area, where the guests spent their recreational time when exploring. The light, airy room, which had been created from two of the original downstairs rooms, had recently been redecorated with wallpaper featuring small, yellow, spring flowers, Behind the bar, the wall was painted apple green and served as a pleasant contrast. Several tables and chairs were positioned close to the bar, but the main space was dominated by comfortably furnished armchairs and sofas, and an ancient wooden framed television set sitting on a low table in the corner.

Lucy sat at a window table, overlooking the garden with Matt and James, while Lorna sought Maggie. She returned a few minutes later with John Ryan and his team.

Immediately taking charge of the proceedings, Ryan instructed two of his colleagues to move a second table to extend the one where the two boys and Lucy already sat, and then asked Maggie to introduce the young boatmen.

Maggie warmly presented Matt and James, explaining how reliable they were, and that despite their youth, nobody knew the loch better, or spent more time upon it.

Ryan had a ready smile, although its apparent warmth failed to reach his eyes, which remained inscrutable, rather like a snake's. His handshake was unexpectedly weak, as if he didn't particularly like this social ritual, offering physical contact to others, and his verbal greeting, brief and formal.

He introduced his three colleagues one at a time, briefly describing the role they played within his team. Two of them, however, seemed much warmer than John Ryan himself. Marty Johnson, a sonar expert and fellow American. A likeable man, fresh from university. Pete Jackson, the group's research assistant and photographic genius, a man in his early thirties who had friendly eyes and rather long, blond hair, and who looked as if he would be quite at home on a surfboard. Finally, the balding, sour-looking man in his forties, introduced as "David Heart, the chief gofer." He didn't seem to enjoy the description and visibly scowled as it was used, but he smiled at the boys and gave a friendly nod.

Ryan wasted no time in unfolding a large-scale map of the loch depicting the seven tributaries and its one outlet, the River Ness. Already drawn on the map, a series of red lines stretched along its twenty-three-mile length.

"These are the sweep lines we've plotted to sonar the bottom of the entire loch. Due to its shape, some sweeps are shorter than others, but I estimate that in the boat you have, it will take approximately two weeks to complete the task. After that, smaller scale studies need completing, where past sightings were reported, and will take a further two-week period. Possibly diving at various locations, but minimised because of the loch's depth. How reliable is your boat?" asked Ryan, finishing abruptly.

Maggie answered for the boys. "The boat's in excellent shape, an' the engine was serviced earlier in the year, but gettin' enough diesel tae run it can be problematic. As ye no doubt noted on yer journey up, there are nae garages aroun' here, so we usually have it brought in by tanker and stored in a five-hundred-gallon tank, some two hundred yards from the boat's moorins', for safety reasons. It's also the nearest the tanker can get tae the boat!" she smiled.

"Do these men ever speak for themselves?" Ryan asked, rather rudely.

"Maggie is our manager," interjected Matt, before Maggie could answer. "She handles the formal side of our business, freeing us to tackle the physical work. She is always welcome to speak on our behalf."

"One other thing, Mr Ryan. I expect you to remain courteous to Maggie at all times; that way, we'll get along just fine," said James, staring hard into Ryan's eyes, angered at his tone towards her.

Looking rather taken aback at their response, Ryan hesitated. "Sorry if I sounded a little abrupt. I know the American manner can be misinterpreted in other places; we often unwittingly get bad press for our forthrightness. I'm newly arrived in your country and am not quite familiar with the quaint, old ways of 'Bonnie Scotland'. I really meant no offence," he apologised, even though his eyes showed not a glimmer of remorse.

"Nae harm done!" said Maggie breezily, though now feeling even more offended.

The discussion changed, focusing on the daily duration of time required for the boat, and the nutritional requirements of the team. Maggie explained that this would all be taken care of by her; food, prepared in the morning before departure, would require little cooking. The evening meal times could be adjusted, suiting the working day length, and all were invited to eat at the house. Everyone appeared satisfied.

Discussing matters of the boat, Matt told Ryan that, although he could use the wheelhouse to monitor operations, only two were allowed inside because of limited space. The deck was free for them to use at will, and for stowing equipment, but the downstairs living space remained strictly out of bounds. Ryan appeared content, but wanted to check the amount of space on deck. He nodded thoughtfully when James informed the deck was completely clear except for the rarely used winch, as all the old fishing gear had been removed many years ago. He had a great deal of bulky equipment and showed concern about the security. He became placated after hearing that the boys lived on board during the summer and that the equipment could be covered in tarpaulins and fastened down securely.

"Now that that's all settled," continued Ryan, "We'll start bringing our gear aboard this afternoon, so we can make an early start in the morning. Be ready to depart at 8.30 and we'll finish as near as dammit at 5.30, at the end of one of the sonar sweeps, if that's agreeable?"

Then he nodded abruptly, stood and left the room, leaving the others perplexed.

An uncomfortable momentary silence hung in the air. Nobody wanted to comment and yet they all shared similar opinion of John Ryan, and it was not a favourable one.

After the meeting, Maggie sent the twins along with the boys to help Ryan and his team load the equipment onto the boat. They set off straight away as they were walking, while Ryan's team shared a van. The four friends shared their feelings of instant dislike for Ryan and Heart, but agreed that there was some hope, at least, in Marty and Pete.

They reached the boat as Ryan appeared with the first of several loads. Matt showed him briefly around it, while James supervised the positioning of the equipment. The men insisted on unloading particular equipment themselves, explaining its sensitive nature and need for handling with care.

The sonar instruments were housed in the wheelhouse, where Marty and Ryan set up the monitors, running connecting cables outside to be coupled to the device. The underwater detector was shaped like a miniature torpedo, with a small propeller that tilted in all directions at the rear, giving it complete directional movement. It was driven by several large batteries that would be charged overnight by a generator using the same diesel fuel as the boat. Marty connected the cables to it and tested the sonar's motor; it whirred into action, and he checked the movement of the propeller. Giving a thumbs-up to Ryan who had remained in the wheelhouse, he turned and smiled at James.

"Looks like we're good to go," he said. "Let the adventure begin!"

The unloading took a further two hours, and the sun was already setting as they finished. Ryan's crew drove back to the boarding house, while the rest of them walked.

"Hopefully, after our meal tonight, we'll socialise with these people and become more acquainted before heading out tomorrow," said Matt, to nobody in particular.

"I reckon we should get the girls to do a little flirting to help loosen them up a bit," suggested James, getting a playful slap from Lucy in return.

"We won't need to go that far, thank you kindly, Jimmy! Maggie's serving up some more of that venison stew tonight, along with her special Rumbledelthumps recipe, and is opening a bottle of her finest malt whisky. I reckon, after a hearty Scottish meal and an hour of drinking, they'll chat just fine!" said Lorna.

"I do hope so. Two of them seem to be most unfriendly, in fact, almost hostile, if you ask me," added Lucy.

"Well, it gives us a chance to work on them then," James stated optimistically.

Chapter 6:
The First Day

At 8.30 sharp the following morning, the team boarded the Matthew James. Ryan barked an order at Matt to get the boat underway and James untied the tethers. Matt started the engine.

When James had jumped back on board, Matt slipped the gear lever forward one position, increased the engine's revolutions and spun the ship's wheel as the boat moved slowly away from its mooring. Once clear, he slipped the gear lever into second, allowing the boat to pick up speed, pleased to discover he could do something he had never knowingly done before.

The others remained on deck, but Ryan observed Matt carefully from the wheelhouse, before unrolling a chart on the small table, and weighing down the corners to prevent it from rolling up again. He pointed to an area at the bottom of the map, the southern-most point of the loch, near Fort Augustus, and instructed Matt to adopt a straight course there, and asking for a time estimate.

Matt, of course, had no real idea but suggested an hour,

depending on the developing wind that was increasing in strength. It sounded completely plausible, so convincing, in fact, that he even believed it himself!

Leaving the wheelhouse, Ryan told Marty to hook up the sonar and prepare it for launch. Preparations were finished just as the boat reached its first destination. Studying the map, Matt followed the red line from Fort Augustus up to the top of the map and saw that this first sweep ended at Dores at the north-east end of the loch, a distance of 18 nautical miles.

Nautical was a foreign word to Matt, but he knew a nautical mile was further than a conventional mile. Since his speed was measured in knots, which he understood even less about, he couldn't estimate how long each sweep would take, and hoped Ryan wouldn't ask.

He needn't have worried, because when Ryan returned, closely followed by James, he asked Matt to wait until the team were ready and then proceed at six knots along the chart-marked line.

Ryan was sitting at the table when Marty arrived to turn on the sonar equipment. He gave a signal through the wheelhouse window to Heart, who lifted the torpedo-shaped device over the side and lowered it gently into the water, while Pete held on to his belt as he over-extended his body and threatened to slip into the water himself. The sonar's propeller started to spin and Marty eased it forward, increasing the angle of pitch so that it dipped below the surface of the loch and announced to Ryan that they were ready. Matt moved forward and spun the ship's wheel until the compass read zero two zero degrees and increased the throttle until the speedometer read six knots. Ryan grunted his approval after Marty declared that everything was working correctly and that the ship's speed and direction were perfect.

From his position alongside Matt, James watched the visual image of the loch bottom appearing on the monitor screen, now removed from the shelf to the table. The loch bottom appeared completely flat with few features of note. Marty saw him concentrating and pointed out heavy concentrations of fish that appeared on the screen in patches of small dots.

"Looks like your fish stocks are healthy here," he said warmly, trying to open up the conversation.

"Not exactly expected if you're trying to prove the existence of a monster. Since fish would be the most likely source of food for such a creature, I was hoping to see rather fewer of them," said Ryan, scowling at the early discoveries revealed by the sonar.

James contributed his thoughts on the matter. "Surely if a monster exists, plentiful food stocks would be needed. When you consider, this creature, sighted and documented for the past thirty-five years, could theoretically still be living. A lack of food would surely lead to its ultimate demise, wouldn't it?"

"Just concentrate on the boat and leave the science to the experts, boy!" snapped Ryan, disliking the fact that James had challenged his authority, and immediately ending any further discussion.

James turned away, glancing at Matt and raised his eyebrows, but his friend quietly told him to ignore Ryan. Like James, he expected this job would be long and tedious.

It took them nearly three hours to reach their target destination at the end of the loch, as the wind had picked up significantly from the east, hampering the boat's steering as well as her speed. Matt had to constantly make subtle adjustments to keep the boat on line, and Marty commented

43

on his skill with real admiration.

"Maggie said you were the best, I understand why," he told Matt, who received the compliment with pride.

He lined up the boat for the return leg and they moved forward with the minimum of delay, this time using the compass setting of two zero zero degrees and at six knots. They ran for an hour, before the sonar image on the monitor began acting violently.

"Cut the engines!" yelled Marty and disappeared outside at a run.

Matt followed the request, trying to hold their position as best he could against the wind, which was now strong enough to whip the surface of the loch into a dramatic procession of white horses. The boat rocked significantly in its stationary state and, from the wheelhouse, he noticed Marty had ordered the sonar retrieved from the water. As they brought it aboard, a tangled mess of line had clogged up the propeller, causing it to stall. James went outside to offer his help, but the extremely unpleasant Heart ordered him to back off, so he returned to the wheelhouse. Ryan moved to inspect the damage and his animated state clarified that he was not at all happy.

The boys observed as they freed the propeller from its unwanted burden, cutting it carefully with knives. Then, after what appeared to be a major argument between Marty and Ryan, Marty dismantled the propeller from the device and brought it into the wheelhouse. Ryan followed, rolling up the map on the table to give Marty space to work.

"What's the problem?" asked Matt.

"Looks like we might have damaged the propeller bearing. This is a complex device that requires running at optimal performance, to get worthwhile readings. I can't afford to take that chance, so I'll have to change the bearing.

We have spare parts, but it will take me at least an hour to replace it," Marty replied, calmly.

Despite the apparent row between him and Ryan, Marty clearly was not the sort of man to let things distract him from his purpose.

"Seems the perfect opportunity to break for lunch since we are of little help!" Matt said, retrieving the basket of food Maggie had provided for the trip. The sandwiches were sealed tightly in plastic containers with a name on each of them, as Maggie had adhered to the individual requests of her guests. James handed out the containers and disappeared below to brew coffee.

The repairs took over two hours and Ryan fumed about the delay. He had resorted to mouthing obscenities, directed at Marty, whilst pacing continually around the deck. Matt commented on Ryan's lack of self-control to James, which Marty overheard.

"You ain't seen nothing yet, wait till he gets furious!" he told them.

Matt just raised his eyebrows whilst James rolled his eyes towards heaven.

The propeller was eventually mounted back onto the device, and Ryan cursed even more when Marty insisted that he carry out a series of tests on the equipment before they resumed the sweeps. Marty said nothing, knowing this would infuriate Ryan further and was fair payback for the earlier insults.

Returning to the wheelhouse, he winked at Matt as if confirming the delay was deliberate, and Matt smiled as he lined up the boat to get underway. To worsen the situation, Marty insisted, after the sweep's conclusion, on conducting more tests before attempting further sweeps. Basically, announcing the day's final run.

Ryan exploded when Marty explained, sounding off a string of obscenities most people would flee from. Marty patiently waited for Ryan to conclude his insults before suggesting he was free to seek another better suited for the job. Ryan grabbed him by the shirt collar and screamed at him not to talk to him like that, but Marty kept his cool, placing his hand on Ryan's and slowly bending his fingers back until Ryan was forced to release him.

"Touch me again, Ryan, and I promise that you'll be swimming with the sonar," Marty said, completely calm and unruffled, and Ryan turned his back and resumed pacing the deck.

"This day improves by the minute, Matt," said James with a shrug.

"Yes, the weeks are certainly going to be a long," agreed Matt, grimly.

"I like Marty, though. I like the way he stands his ground and doesn't take this rubbish from Ryan."

"The others don't appear to hold much importance here, do they?"

"You're right, but it's early days yet and their involvement might increase, especially when you consider that the sonar mapping is only half of what they want to achieve here."

Their conversation was interrupted by Marty's return.

"Say boys, do you know a quiet spot where I can check my equipment without interruption or be bothered by the new Loch Ness Monster?" he asked with a grin.

James grinned back at Ryan's new moniker and offered him the chance to stay on the boat and work, providing he was finished by the time they returned from Maggie's after the evening meal. Marty looked surprised and pleased by the offer, thanking them both warmly. James told him that Maggie would keep something hot for when he returned, whatever the time was.

The rest of the sweep happened according to plan and when they moored the old trawler, Ryan, Heart and Jackson left abruptly without a word, taking the vehicle they had arrived in, without offering the boys a lift.

"Looks like we're walking back," said James, bemused at the attitude shown towards him and Matt.

"Don't take it personally, boys. He's like that with everybody he works with. Nothing, and nobody, is as important as the great John Ryan," Marty laughed.

"You don't like him much, do you?"

"To me, this is just work. I excel at what I do, and he knows it. He pays well, so I can afford to ignore his silly tantrums. You're right though, I don't like him."

James asked him below and showed the living quarters.

"If you want to work below instead of the wheelhouse, it's ok with us. You'll find a supply of coffee and biscuits in the tins to keep hunger at bay. And, if you're not too late, you're welcome to eat with us, if you fancy some warmer company than your employer's."

"Thanks, James, I really appreciate that and I'll take you up on your offer. What time is dinner anyway?"

"Seven o'clock sharp. Will you be finished by then?"

"I'll make sure I am," he replied.

Matt and James left for Maggie's, believing they had made positive moves towards a new friendship.

Chapter 7:
Sonar Contact

Ryan and his colleagues had retired to their rooms by the time the boys returned to the boarding house. Wanting Maggie's impression of the day's events, they immediately joined her in the kitchen.

Maggie was unimpressed with Ryan's behaviour and warned the boys to steer clear of him where possible. She seemed happier with Marty though, especially when she heard that he would be joining them for dinner. She could not join them as she was managing the bar after dinner, on duty until the guests retired for the night.

Secretly, she worried for the boys; taking an instant dislike to Ryan on their first meeting and, after hearing about his exploits today, her maternal instinct towards the two lads were raised. With just a few moments to spare before dinner, Marty arrived, dashing upstairs to wash and change into clean clothes. He soon joined them at the kitchen table with a grin and an apology for cutting it so fine with the time.

The twins also made a late appearance, after running some errands for Maggie in the village. The group fell into comfortable companionship, sharing amusing anecdotes as they consolidated their new relationships. They discovered Marty had learnt his trade in the marines and, after leaving the Navy prematurely. Having built his own sonar device, he wanted to become a freelance sonar operator. He now worked for different oil companies and nautical survey teams. Ryan heard of his innovative services and immediately hired him for mapping the waters of Loch Ness.

Matt asked him about David Heart, but Marty knew little, he had met him days prior to starting the job, and he proved to be an enigma. Marty said he his real purpose here remained unclear, for he had no real job title and didn't appear to do much, at least so far, he was supposed to be proficient at logistics and supplies. Cold and distant, he made no attempt at forming positive relationships with the rest of the crew, and spent more time with Ryan than anybody else. Marty clarified that he didn't particularly like him and would certainly not trust him, but added that this was a gut instinct rather than any solid reasoning.

Marty said that he and Pete Jackson hit it off immediately. Though he was a quiet man, with a keen sense of humour, he didn't relish the idea of working for Ryan, a man whose reputation preceded him. A successful author of several books on the unusual, his main task was collecting evidence from the locals, photographing the area and producing a factual record of Ryan's survey.

James hoped Marty would stay for the duration of the charter and not leave after the sonar sweeps, and was pleased when he learnt the man's hire lasted for the whole month, in case any surveys needed to be repeated. He wasn't expecting any need for that, if his sonar device proved reliable over the

49

two-week period.

The following morning Ryan requested the girls to take Heart and Jackson to Achnahannet to meet the Nessie-watchers of the Local PhBI. Excited at the prospect of being involved, they took the dinghy out early, leaving before Matt and James appeared on deck.

The second day's sweep would run parallel courses to the first, and with a lighter wind, Ryan hoped for several complete runs. The first ran smoothly, with James helping Marty to launch the sonar device, and they took a fifteen-minute break to eat lunch before starting the second run.

Halfway through the sweep, Marty called out to Ryan, saying that a large moving shape followed the boat below them. Ryan stared at the monitor, observing.

"Speed?" he asked, curtly.

"Matching our own, at about six knots," answered Marty.

"Depth?"

"Sixty-five feet at present but varying between fifty and eighty feet."

"Size?"

"Approximately twenty-five to thirty feet long."

James watched the monitor frequently and could easily distinguish the shape they observed from the other blotches of fish shoals. He felt the excitement and anticipation of the hunt.

Keeping his eyes firmly on the compass, Matt ensured that their line of travel maintained the high level of accuracy expected of him.

"It definitely seems to be following the boat," Marty said after observing for a full five minutes.

"There's no variation in its course at all, but its depth

is constantly changing," said Ryan, continuing to stare at the monitor.

"Interesting!"

As he spoke, whatever moved below them veered off suddenly and was lost from the monitor.

"Did we get all that on tape?" he asked Marty. "Everything we see is automatically recorded and can be played back at your convenience," Marty told him.

Ryan left the wheelhouse and patrolled the deck. He stood staring at both sides of the loch as if taking visual references to their position. He pulled a notebook from his pocket and started notating, before returning to the wheelhouse without speaking.

They travelled for another two miles, when the mysterious shape reappeared on the monitor screen. Marty didn't need to announce it this time, for Ryan and James were already studying the screen intently and observed the creature for themselves.

Marty called the depth and speed as the creature followed the boat. Again, Ryan moved outside and took notes about the visual location before returning, monitoring the screen and then repeating the note-making when the shape veered off after a mile.

James looked at Marty. "Any ideas what it could be?" he asked, but Marty shook his head.

"Not a clue!"

On the return leg, although everyone watched intently, but no further contact with the mysterious object occurred and the whole run was made in complete silence.

As they moored the boat, Marty informed them he would be staying on board again to check his equipment, but was told by Ryan that attending the meeting at six that evening was expected. Matt and James received a request to be there too. Matt reminded him of their need for diesel, but Ryan suggested refilling the boat's fuel tank early the next morning and left, leaving the boys to walk back to the boarding house.

Once everyone disappeared from sight, Marty admitted the need to check his equipment was a ruse; he just wanted to avoid being alone with Ryan. The boys said nothing but secretly empathised with him. Marty offered to help with the tasks on board before leaving for Maggie's, with an hour to pass before attending for the meeting.

With little to do they sat on deck in the late afternoon sunlight discussing the day's events. Marty asked if they believed in Nessie, the boys gave their honest opinions. Their new friend understood, telling them that since becoming a sonar operator, he witnessed strange things in oceans all around the world; readings suggesting large creatures existed in the most unexpected of places but, despite this, no concrete evidence was found to confirm his readings.

"So, you see boys, I find myself of the same opinion as you. There is definitely something present, but I need evidence beyond the sonar readings."

The three walked briskly to Maggie's, pleased to stretch their legs after the confinement on the boat. Arriving for the meeting with a few minutes to spare, they were surprised to see Ryan tapping his fingers with annoyance. Perhaps annoyed that they hadn't shown more respect by already arriving and waiting for him, but they ignored his unspoken protest and sat down together. The twins had returned earlier and sat at the table with Heart and Jackson.

"We've all finally arrived!" Ryan began, before interrupted by Marty who added, "On time too!"

James looked away to prevent Ryan seeing the amusement on his face, and Matt stifled a laugh with a fictitious coughing fit.

Ryan glared at Marty, before continuing, "Because of today's events, there's a change of plan for tomorrow… Heart will be onshore, organising supplies for the next stage of our project. On the boat, same crew as today, the girls will escort Jackson to these four locations to install time-lapse photography stations. Two on both sides of the loch, a lengthy day, but everyone meets at six o'clock tomorrow evening for briefing. Questions?"

Nobody replied and Ryan declared an end to the meeting, three minutes after starting. All of Ryan's crew left for their rooms, leaving Matt, James and the twins to share their stories of the day.

The girls' day was uneventful but worrying. Jackson had befriended the girls, and they were comfortable in his presence, but Heart dominated their time. He was as rude to them as Ryan was towards the boys. He asked to be shown the observation point to take photographs and, upon learning three other observation points existed, he insisted on visiting all of them. The girls asked what he photographed and were told that it did not concern them. He informed them that their job was to ferry Jackson and him around, as required, and that he had no intention of justifying his actions to mere taxi drivers.

Feeling quite indignant about this, James suggested that the pairs split up, with Lucy going on the boat with Matt, whilst he accompanied Lorna on the dinghy. Both girls initially liked this idea, but didn't want to risk upsetting the clients and possibly jeopardising their boat-hire business, so said they would give him another chance.

"I won't allow any client to treat us like that, business

or no business," said James, and warned that, if this callous attitude toward them continued, they would definitely be swapping their pairings.

As Maggie prepared the evening meal, Matt asked her opinion, and she agreed they should give them one more chance but she would confront Ryan about Heart's attitude.

Somehow though, Matt doubted it would make a difference and declared, if confronting was necessary, he would deal with it.

Marty didn't join them for dinner that night, electing to eat alone in his room. Matt and James ate with the twins until Lorna relieved Maggie from her duties at the bar, so that she could sit with them.

Throughout dinner, Maggie surreptitiously observed Ryan and his men, listening to their conversation. Her reservations about the group were such, that she was half-expecting something unpleasant to happen, although no idea what. After the meal, she discussed this with the boys, finding that they shared her sense of unease. In a busier year, they would have encouraged Ryan to leave, but employment was limited, and losing it because of poor first impressions was frivolous. All agreed their guest's behaviour would not be tolerated for the entire month.

Chapter 8:
Could It Really Be Nessie?

Jackson met the twins early the following morning, knowing a lot of work lay ahead that day. As they set off, they all felt relieved that Heart wasn't with them to spoil the amicable atmosphere as they strolled towards the dinghy.

Jackson needed to collect his photography equipment from the boat, which gave them the opportunity to discuss tactics as they loaded the dinghy. They decided to seek the locations on the opposite side of the lock first, and knowing that two different points were opposite and approximately two miles apart, they could follow the route on a similar sonar sweep line the boys used the previous day. Realising it would take a half-hour to reach the initial location point, the girls took turns at the tiller between each.

It was a quiet morning and just before they left; they studied the notes that Ryan had made yesterday. They instantly recognised the first description; the shape of a rocky outcrop, clearly distinguishable from the detail written down. The second location was less obvious but, aware of its approximation two miles further, Lorna did not estimate problems discovering it. Lucy started the engine and the little outboard motor kicked into action.

Jackson untied the mooring rope, and they set off across the loch at a comfortable speed.

They enjoyed the coolness of the air across their faces, and the sight of the water shimmering in the early morning sun, which didn't catch the caress of the breeze that usually rippled its surface. The promise of another beautiful day, stimulated a sense of joy and vibrance at being alive. The twins kept an eye out for bird life as they travelled and viewed a pair of ospreys wheeling high in the sky, gliding in lazy circles on a thermal; and a cormorant standing on the shoreline, with its wings outspread in the sun.

"Did you know that cormorants are the only web- footed birds that don't produce a waterproof oil for their feathers? So, after swimming underwater, they dry them off before flying off again," Lorna told Jackson in her lilting voice as they passed by.

"I certainly didn't know that! But I lacked the opportunities for serious bird-watching you experienced growing up in this gorgeous landscape."

He had picked up one of his cameras as he spoke, and after making a few swift adjustments to lens and shutter, took several shots of the waterbird.

"I'll send you a copy to show to other townies who come to visit!" he said with a smile.

"First location, coming up!" Lucy announced and reduced the speed of the boat. Using the rocky outcrop reference from Ryan's notes, they had arrived at the far side of the loch where they moored the boat and unloaded Jackson's equipment, asking him where he wanted to set up the camera.

"High elevation will be best," he told them.

The terrain was steep, and ascending hard work, carrying risk of falling and injury.

"If my memory serves me right, there's a small trail here somewhere, leading about halfway up. Following it will make some of the climb easier with the equipment. Been years since I was here, but my memory is excellent and I'm positively sure," Lucy told him.

"Let's scout around then and search for it.

There's quite a lot of gear to carry," said Jackson.

Lorna discovered the path after searching for only a few minutes, so they loaded up the camera equipment and started to walk uphill.

"How high do we need to travel, Mr. Jackson?" Lorna asked, as they followed the twisting path upward.

"Please call me Pete!" he replied with a friendly smile.

"Any location with a clear view, between three and five hundred feet high would be good."

"That's good news, because this path goes higher than that, which means we won't climb the more difficult slopes at the top," said Lucy.

"Where exactly does this path lead?" asked Pete.

"To a scree slope further up. There are some huge rocks amongst the scree and ornithologists like to camp there for cover when photographing," Lucy informed him.

"Sounds like the perfect place," said Pete, grinning at the news.

"Yes, in dry weather, when wet, the path is rather treacherous. There have been a few accidents involving broken limbs in the past," she continued.

After another ten minutes, they reached the base of the scree and the path finished. The view of the loch was exceptional and, as they stared, they witnessed the Matthew James travelling below on one of many relays on the long stretch of water.

Jackson selected a large rock about ten yards further up the scree slope on which to mount his camera, and placed it with precision, checking the viewfinder several times.

The girls watched him work without interrupting, and he seemed to appreciate their restraint. When he was confident the camera was correctly placed, Pete asked Lorna to open a rucksack and withdraw a roll of adhesive tape, which he used to secure the camera to the rock.

Conducting the final checks, he turned it on. "One down, three to go!" he announced, satisfied.

Lucy took a large bottle of water from her pack and poured some into three small cups, passing them around. They sat looking at the loch for a few minutes, slowly sipping the cool drink, enjoying the panoramic view. The perfect, peaceful setting, and for Lucy and Lorna representing both their home and their way of life.

They compared the possibility of hiking the two miles to the next location to using the dinghy again. Both girls considered the equipment that required carrying, suggesting the journey would be easier by boat, and Pete was happy to acquiesce, so they head downhill, back to the boat.

The second location was well concealed from their position, and they resorted to matching the reference for the opposite side of the loch to achieve its approximation. The route was tough, lacking trails to follow, and they constantly dodged trees and boulders. There, they eventually discovered a small clearing at the approximate height Pete required for his camera position.

Underfoot, the ground was covered in loose, decaying branches and pine cones, and the soil itself was dusty and slippery, taking them twice as long as expected to reach the clearing which was just as high as their previous spot had been. The clearing was much larger than appeared from the dinghy's perspective and, with an absence of rocks or other features within, Pete selected a tree at the rear to mount his camera. This would give him some additional height to scan over the woodland below, and he climbed the sturdy trunk about ten feet up to get the view he needed. Unrolling a length of tape, he attached the camera between at a fork in the branches About to switch on, something in the loch caught his eye.

He called the girls who turned toward the direction his finger pointed. Pete turned on the camera, swung down from the tree and retrieved a pair of powerful binoculars from his rucksack. He turned the wheel between the lenses slowly, focusing on the moving object, before gasping in surprise.

Lucy grabbed her own pair and followed his lead. She let out a small squeal and passed them to her sister who finally spoke.

"That couldn't be Nessie, could it?"

As they watched, the mysterious shape skimmed along the surface of the water, submerging and reappearing at regular intervals. They experienced difficulty gauging the size from so far away, but it was clearly substantial; the dark, elongated hump leaving a white, almost phosphorescent wake behind. They followed the creature's progress up the loch in silence and awe until, abruptly, it disappeared below the surface, leaving them saddened and with a sense of loss that they could not explain.

Lorna broke the silence first. "Did we really see that? Was that really Nessie?"

Pete looked at her with excitement written all over his face.

"I can't imagine what else might explain that. And it will need explaining because I've just filmed it. I'd better change this roll of film before we set up the others, so we can take the evidence to Ryan. Boy, he'll be annoyed he didn't sight it first!"

They made their way excitedly back to the dinghy where Lorna took the tiller. Starting the engine, she steered the craft across the loch to the opposite bank. Seeing Nessie had lifted their mood, they were buoyant, and there was more banter between them than usual.

They landed and began the third leg of their task, finding the location effortlessly and while Pete mounted the next camera, both girls sat with the binoculars glued to their eyes, anticipating the creature reappearing, but they waited in vain. They saw the Matthew James though, making its final sweep back towards their starting point. They both waved madly, to Pete's obvious amusement, but it was unlikely that they would be seen against the dense backdrop of the forest.

At five to seven they finally reached Maggie's, ending an exhausting day of hiking with heavy equipment. Pete rushed to develop the film before the meeting. As they trooped into the lounge, Ryan looked ready to explode, his impatience totally exhausted He was just opening his mouth to speak, when Matt rushed over to them, saying how worried he had been that they were so late. He was convinced they'd experienced an accident, or the outboard had packed up.

He wasn't really worried in the slightest, just trying to prevent Ryan's imminent outburst. The ploy worked. Pete offered apologies, explaining he had film they should see immediately.

His anger now overridden by his curiosity at Jackson and the twins' evident excitement, Ryan watched the preparations with impatient interest as Pete plugged in the projector, unrolled and erected a white screen, while Lorna switched off the lights.

The lock image appeared on the screen with a dark object in the water visible, moving smoothly through the water.

Maggie came in to announce dinner was ready to serve, but stopped immediately when seeing the projected image. She stared with wide eyes, then abruptly turned and left.

Noticing her reaction, James discreetly followed her out.

"Maggie! Are you ok? You left so quickly!"

I cannae believe what I've just seen," she told him. "The creature I witnessed so long ago. That's Nessie!"

James stared at her with shining eyes. "Then it's true, she really *does* exist!"

Chapter 9:
Change of Tack

James returned to the meeting just as Ryan was summing up his initial thoughts of the film they'd been shown.

"In my opinion, the sighting verifies the existence of a plesiosaur in the loch; the most likely explanation, and reinforces some earlier sightings. The size and proportions seem to support my early conclusions and the fact that it can survive in extremely deep water suggest that it has extraordinary capabilities that quite rule out any other creatures. Considering the loch is deeper than the North Sea in places, it's understandable why sightings through the decades were sporadic

"I am, as yet, unable to the dismiss the possibility that the creature can come onto dry land, although science would suggest otherwise, thus discredit the land sightings. Knowing the bottom of the loch is flat and devoid of plant life, the natural assumption suggests the creature is piscivorous.

Seven tributaries supply the loch and only one outlet, which means it's constantly being replenished, and explains why the fish stocks are healthy, despite supporting such a substantial creature.

"Because of these findings, so early in our investigation, I'll be making a few alterations to our schedule, a slight 'change of tack' if you like. For the immediate future, I want to finish the sonar exploration. Our task now is discovering the most likely places this creature might inhabit within the loch. While we explore this through the sonar mapping, I want Jackson to scout another location, three miles north of today's position, and set up cameras on both sides of the lake. Heart, you'll be purchasing several special supplies for me and instigating the supply of a net large enough and strong enough to hold the creature when we catch it. Ladies, you will accompany Jackson, of course. Your knowledge of the local terrain is invaluable to the project, and your boating skills.

"Excellent work today people, let's keep the momentum going. That's it! Questions?"

Matt looked hard at Ryan and asked the question on everybody's mind.

"How do you propose to catch a creature of this size, especially as it swims as fast as the boat, possibly faster?"

"That's a sensible question and I'll be considering one or two ideas. There are options and I'll deliberate before discussing my conclusions later, after the sonar mapping has finished," Ryan said, finishing the longest speech that they had ever heard him make.

The rest of the week passed uneventfully, no sightings of the plesiosaur, and as the sonar mapping approached the halfway stage, no further sonar contact. Ryan refrained from saying much during the evening meetings, now lasting less than five minutes, too distracted by whatever plans he was working on. He rarely left his room once they returned from the boats, even taking his meals upstairs, which the others considered something of a relief.

Maggie had become avidly interested in all the goings on since the first sighting. She attended the daily meetings and insisted on hearing the finer details from Matt, James and the twins, explaining away her interest with the updating of her scrapbooks. They were happy to share the day's events with her as they ate the evening meals, and enjoy each other's company as they chatted or played cards together at the long wooden table.

Heart made the lengthy journey to Edinburgh, returning with a net so large, it required transporting on a small, flat-bed lorry. He left it at the mooring place of the Matthew James. The netting was made of a strong, nylon rope and its entirety was massive. When required, they would unload the majority of Ryan's equipment to make room on the Matthew James' deck. Since most of the boat's original fishing equipment had been removed from the ageing trawler, it wasn't clear how the net would be deployed from the boat.

Much to the relief of the twins, Heart had taken to joining his boss on the trawler each day, having finished the tasks that Ryan had set him.

The second week started with a familiar routine, and on Monday afternoon the creature appeared on the sonar screen again, at roughly a similar depth as before. Again, it followed the boat for approximately two miles before disappearing off the monitor screen.

Ryan halted the sweep and asked Matt to steer the boat in increasing large circles to discover where it had gone. He became angry when they could see no sign of it, and took his frustration out on Marty, insulting the quality of his equipment. Marty took the abuse with apparent disregard, thus exacerbating the angry man's outburst, but when Ryan left the wheelhouse to speak to Heart, Marty looked at Matt and James, saying simply,

"The man's an idiot with no regard for anyone but himself."

They grinned at him, and Marty explained that although it was rather like searching for a needle in a haystack, without his equipment they wouldn't know which field the haystack was in!

During the return leg, Nessie reappeared on the screen in the same location as earlier. Ryan immediately gave the order to follow it when it veered off from their direct path. Matt asked Marty to call the correct bearing to follow when the creature left so he could concentrate on steering rather than staring at the monitor.

"Half speed!" called Ryan, his excitement rising. "Let's see if the creature is intelligent enough to mirror our speed when we change it!"

As the boat reduced its speed, Marty called out that the creature was maintaining its distance behind them.

"Three-quarter speed and keep it steady!"

Again, the creature increased its own speed to match that of the boat. Ryan watched the monitor intently. He gave the instruction to bear five degrees starboard. Once more, the creature kept pace and direction with them.

"Maintain present course and speed," Ryan barked and went outside to Heart who was standing on deck looking out into the murky depths of the water.

James saw excited words were being spoken between the two through the wheelhouse window. He watched as Heart uncovered the pile of equipment and removed a piece of machinery about three feet square and two feet tall. There was a heavy spring within its framework and a retaining mechanism attached to two lever-like arms. Heart pulled backwards on the retaining mechanism and the arms moved backwards towards him, clicking into position.

James looked at Matt with questioning eyes, asking wordlessly what Heart was up to, but Matt just shrugged, his eyes moving quickly back to the compass as he tried to ensure the boat ran straight and true.

Ryan appeared momentarily by the wheelhouse, asking for the current depth of the creature and relayed the information back to his associate.

Opening a heavy wooden crate, Heart removed one of a dozen metal cylinders, which he loaded between the two metal arms of the equipment. Positioning the device so it was pointing at the wheelhouse, he raised his thumb to Ryan, who checked the monitor screen before leaving to join him. Heart crouched down behind the device until Ryan finally gave him a small nod, before pushing the release button. The arms shot forward, armed by the large spring and launched the cylinder forward, straight over the wheelhouse to land about fifty feet behind the boat. James involuntarily ducked as it passed overhead.

"What was that?" he asked Matt, before a strange, muffled rumble rippled through the boat and a colossal plume of water erupted into the air.

Before Matt could offer an answer Marty interrupted.

"What the hell was that?" Marty yelled, his eyes leaving the monitor.

James explained what he had seen and saw the rage erupt on Marty's normally peaceful face.

"Depth charges! The idiots, they're using depth charges!

He'll stop at nothing until he wrecks my equipment and blows us out of the water!" he shouted incredulously. "James, you'd better help me retrieve the equipment from the water before he destroys it. Matt, I suggest you stop the boat."

Marty strode outside, with James following.

"Ryan, have you lost your mind, you stupid idiot?" he asked, going straight up to him and standing just inches from him. "You could destroy all the sensitive components in the sonar, not to mention the danger risked to the boat."

"Now, Marty, you're exaggerating. The charge was a safe distance from sonar and boat. Heart's an expert with these devices, absolutely no danger," said Ryan calmly, trying to relieve the tension.

"What about the danger to the creature?" asked James. "What gives you the right to harm it? What makes you think you can play God and decide its fate? It's done nothing to harm anyone," he continued, angrily.

"My permit surveying the loch and investigating the phenomenon of the Loch Ness Monster gives me the right, and it's my choice to select any method at my disposal to achieve solving the mystery," said Ryan, angrily, his voice getting more menacing by the second. "I've invested thousands of dollars into this venture and I intend to show Nessie to the world, dead or alive."

Marty took a step forward and shot out his fist in a perfect uppercut that connected to Ryan's chin. The force of it lifted Ryan into the air and sent him sprawling into a heap of tangled arms and legs against the pile of rope netting, where he lay unmoving. Next, Marty turned his attention towards Heart and took a step towards him. Heart saw his intention, reached inside his jacket and pulled out a gun.

"Take one more step, and I promise you it'll be your last," he said, pointing the weapon at Marty's chest. There was a momentary silence as Marty weighed up his options, but remained perfectly still.

It was James who broke the silence. "What the hell?" he questioned excitedly, pointing to a spot in the lake.

Heart fell for the oldest trick in the book, turning his head to where James was pointing. As he did so, both James and Marty launched themselves forward in tandem, hitting Heart's body full-on and sending him over the side of the boat and into the water, the gun flying from his hand and disappearing into the depths. Marty grabbed the net and prevented himself from going overboard too, but James's momentum was too great to check and propelled him into the shocking cold of the loch.

Chapter 10:
Disaster for the Twins

The twins were excited about their trip with Pete, as they would be checking the time-lapse film set the previous week. Their new friend planned to check one side of the loch today and save the other for tomorrow.

Leaving early in the morning, they soon arrived at the first location. They made the climb up to the camera position effortlessly; even Pete was feeling the benefit of the previous week's exertions, and was scarcely out of breath on arrival.

The camera was still firmly attached to the rock where they had left it, so Jackson replaced the film and batteries before putting the exposed film into his bag for developing and viewing later. Securing the camera back to the rock, he spent extra time checking the viewfinder and focus.

As they directed the boat towards the second location, Pete explained about the time-lapse technique that he often used to photograph animals in the wild.

"The camera takes images every five seconds, which are then shown back at twenty-four frames per second, thus seeming to speed up the rate of activity. For every one good clip, you can use up hundreds of hours of film. It requires a lot of patience to do this type of work, and requires solid research and a firm belief that you'll get what you want if you pursue it long enough. So, don't feel disappointed if we don't achieve our aim straight away, girls. Remember, we already have one clear piece of film showing Nessie."

Lorna told him they had complete faith in his objectives and as much patience as needed, but were desperate to view the footage after developing the film.

Lucy slowly maneuvered the dinghy onto the shore and they clambered out on to the fine gravel, securing the small craft to a large rock. The climb was worse than their previous visit, as rain had fallen during the night. This hillside was steep and slippery, and when they finally reached the clearing where the second camera had been placed, they were covered in mud. They responded to their falls with good humour.

Pete tried to climb the tree to retrieve the camera several times but could not get a secure purchase on the slippery trunk and slid down several times before he was forced to give up.

"Why don't one of you stand on my shoulders? I'm sure you'd be able to reach those fatter branches and pull yourself up the last few feet to the camera."

Lorna accepted the challenge, so Pete crouched down in front of the tree for her to place her foot on his shoulder. She grabbed on to the trunk and, with Lucy's support, moved her second foot into position. Pete stood up carefully with his hands around her ankles and she climbed easily into the tree, moving deftly from branch to branch until she could retrieve the camera.

Climbing back down towards Pete, Lorna lowered the camera to her sister before stepping onto his shoulder once more. As she shifted her weight onto it, the mud already on his shoulder caused her foot to slip and with her second foot unsecured, she hurtled backwards and crashed heavily to the ground where she started to slide headfirst down the slope.

Pete and Lucy moved quickly, following her rapid descent, but she came to an abrupt stop before they reached her. Her foot had snagged between two rocks and was twisted at an unnatural angle. She lay there unmoving, moaning softly, and her eyes were closed.

Lucy scuttled to her side. "Lorna, are you alright?" she asked, gently shaking her shoulders.

Lorna didn't move or open her eyes, but moaned loudly. Pete reached into his pack and took out his water bottle and gently trickled a little over Lorna's face. She responded immediately by opening her eyes, wincing at the pain she was feeling.

"Where are you hurt, Lorna?" asked Pete.

She didn't answer immediately, but lay staring at them, blinking her eyes.

Lucy stared at her twin, unable to speak, as she watched her struggling against the pain and shock. Pete stroked Lorna's cheek gently.

"Look at me!" he said, waiting for her to direct her eyes towards his. "It's going to be ok. But you need to tell us where it hurts."

His voice was soft but firm, and, reassuring.

"All over! But mostly my arm and ankle," she finally replied, breathlessly, her voice distorted by the agonising pain.

Pete expertly ran his fingers down the arm she indicated, stopping abruptly when he saw her wince as he felt an unnatural lump. Gently, he pulled her trouser leg up a few inches to see her ankle. He and Lucy made eye contact briefly, sharing their dismay, after seeing the extent of the swelling. Lorna tried to sit up, but Pete put his hands on her shoulders to restrain her.

"Lie still, Lorna! I think you've broken your arm and possibly your ankle. You mustn't move in case you do more damage to them."

69

Then, turning to Lucy, he said. "We need to get help. You should return, get some medics here with a stretcher. We can't move her safely without the proper equipment and you handle the boat better than me."

"I can't leave her! I've got to stay!" Lucy argued. "Lucy, I'll take good care of her," Pete assured her "You know I will. But you must go now! The sooner you go, the sooner you'll be back again."

Lucy steeled herself, kissed her twin on the forehead and took off down the hillside.

Pete and Lorna heard the outboard motor start up a few minutes later and roar into full throttle as Lucy steered the dinghy expertly at maximum speed back towards home.

Lorna lay still and bravely endured the pain which erupted in waves over her. He slipped his rucksack under her head to make her more comfortable and covered her with his anorak, then settled down beside her and talked to her of unusual creatures he had photographed during his career. He told her the cameras he used, at present, were designed by him and he was currently developing an incredibly powerful camera for filming the growth of plants.

Despite the pain, she listened with interest, telling him in return, at his encouragement, how Maggie had adopted her and Lucy at five after their parents were killed in a car crash on holiday in Scotland. And how wonderful she had been to them throughout the years. Maggie had fostered several children in the past, but she and her twin were the only two adopted. Then she explained how she loved living by the loch and how much it meant to her.

An hour passed before Pete heard the buzz of a boat's engine getting progressively louder and waited for the sound to cut out, signaling the arrival of the rescue party at the foot of the slope. Seeing that Lorna was shivering now, indicating that shock was setting in, he kept her talking, giving her a running commentary on the arrival of her rescuers. Despite her pain, she could not resist smiling at his attempt to make the commentary sound like that of a horse race.

And then they were there! Lucy had brought two burly men from the village who worked as part of a rescue team for visitors who got stranded on walking holidays during adverse weather.

She went straight to her twin's side, taking hold of Lorna's hand, while the two men stepped straight into action. They placed padding around her arm, strapping it to her body in the most comfortable position, and secured her foot to protect it from jolts, before wrapping her up warmly in blankets and lifting her onto a stretcher for the return journey.

At the hospital in Inverness, Lorna's injuries were promptly assessed. She was given the good news that her ankle wasn't broken but badly sprained, then had her broken arm reset and plastered under general anesthetic. She was to stay in hospital overnight.

Lucy tried to insist on staying with her, but Pete suggested that Lorna would probably rest more easily knowing her sister was back at home, rather than sitting up all night in a hospital chair.

He made arrangements for a taxi to drive them home and Lucy, was feeling too tired to resist. She had been touched by his refusal to leave them, how he had dealt with the many phone calls home relaying information and arrangements for the car.

Pete Jackson had become quite fond of the twins over the past week and had enjoyed having them with him. He found his paternal instincts triggered and felt quite responsible for them.

In a quiet moment, when Lucy had left for coffee, Lorna called him to her and kissed him on the cheek.

"Thank you for taking care of me and for organising everything.

Pete looked a bit embarrassed as he replied, "You're

welcome."

A tear ran down her cheek at the realisation she would not venture on the loch for the foreseeable future. For her, the adventure seemed over.

"It's just not fair," she sniffed. "We've only just started, I'm going to miss out on everything, now."

"No, no, we won't let that happen!" he told her, sympathetically. "I promise to come and see you each evening when we finish. I'll give you a personal update on everything we've been doing, and if you promise to be a model patient and follow all the doctor's orders, I might even do it in the style of a horse race!"

Chapter 11:
We Call the Shots, Not You!

Matt came running out of the wheelhouse. Everything had happened so quickly, he had been powerless to help, and was shocked to see his best friend disappear overboard.

"Grab that lifebuoy, Marty, throw it to them!" he shouted.

He grabbed another and threw it towards Heart who screamed that he couldn't swim. James grabbed the nearest ring and, pushing it ahead of him, swam over to Heart telling him to hold on to it. Heart didn't seem to hear him in his panic-stricken state, continuing to thrash wildly at the water. His head dipped under, which panicked him further. James grabbed his arm and forced it through the lifebuoy, then kicked them both towards the second one, which lay drifting lazily, a few yards away. He forced Heart's other arm through it.

"You're ok!" he said firmly. "Stop thrashing about! You're safe now."

Realising that fate was not sending him to the bottom, Heart looked around him, calmer now he held something firm. James took hold of one of the lifebuoys and began kicking towards the trawler, where Marty and Matt were leaning over, waiting to pull Heart out of the water. Once he was safely aboard, James took the extended arm of his friend and climbed aboard, too.

"Good work, James!" Matt told him, clapping him on the back. Then, leaning over, he grasped the lifebuoys and returned them to their positions under the gunnels.

"Do you have rope to tie him up, Matt?" asked Marty. "No telling if this lunatic has other concealed weapons, better safe than sorry."

He bound Heart's wrists behind him. The man made no effort to resist, still shocked by his unexpected, cold-water plunge. He was now shivering violently, but Marty felt little compassion. When he'd finished, Matt pointed at Ryan's motionless form.

"What about him?"

"He's out for the count!" Marty told him. "Though we'd better monitor him."

"Let's return and let the police handle this," said Matt, returning to the wheelhouse to restart the engine.

James draped an old blanket round Heart's shaking shoulders. "It's about time you learnt to swim!" he said. "That could have been really nasty."

During the trip back, Marty stayed on deck, keeping a close eye on the two men. James changed into dry clothes and soon joined Matt in the wheelhouse.

"Where can we secure them, James?" asked Matt.

"Take them to Maggie's and get her to call the local police," James replied, decisively.

"It's a shame, because that means we'll lose the work, and I'm convinced Maggie can't afford to," said Matt.

"That's true. But we can't have these lunatics going round trying to blow helpless animals out of the water and pulling guns on the locals," James told him. "These guys seem to think they can do whatever they want. Perhaps in their own country, but it's not happening here!"

Half an hour later, they tied off the boat at the dock. Ryan had come round and was trying to stand, still groggy from Marty's punch. Heart was on his feet now, mouthing off at Marty and insisting that he was untied. His pleas fell on deaf ears.

"The more you scream and shout, the longer I'm going to leave you tied up," Marty told him.

That Ryan had some sort of hold over Heart was obvious, because when he ordered him to keep quiet, the man immediately stopped his complaining, with a look of fury, saying nothing else until they reached the boarding house.

There, James quickly explained the turn of events to Maggie, who moved to the telephone in reception to call the police. She was clearly furious.

When she had finished speaking, she set down the receiver with a sigh. "They're on their way. Ach, it ne'er rains but it pours, I'm afraid."

Gathering the boys, she told them Lorna had been involved in an accident and was staying in hospital, overnight. She really wanted to travel to her, but refused to leave her guests unattended, especially with the latest developments. But Lucy and Pete were there, and promised to ring the minute they received information about her injuries.

As they were waiting for the police to arrive, four local men came into the bar, nodding their greetings at Matt and James before sitting down. They stared at Ryan and Heart, with contempt clearly written on their faces. Gradually, more entered, in pairs or threes, offering greetings and again nodding to Matt and James before sitting down. The silence hung uneasy in the room.

Finally, Maggie entered with an older man, carrying an air of authority. She explained that they were waiting for three others, members of the local police force who would be with them shortly.

Disappearing out into the kitchen, she returned minutes later with large pots of coffee, and another woman carrying a tray of cups and saucers. Pouring the dark-coloured brew into three of the cups, she passed them to Matt, James and Marty who took them gratefully.

She whispered something in Marty's ear as she gave him the mug and he replied, "You're welcome."

Finally, the police officer appeared and the older man who entered with Maggie, stood and spoke in a self-assured manner.

"I think we're all here now, so let's get started. As some of ye may no, have met me afore, I'll introduce ma'self, first. "I am Colonel Alistair Murray, chairman of an ol' society that looks out fur the interest o' the locals who live aroun' Loch Ness. A major concern has been brought tae ma attention that requires an emergency meeting of our society an' I would like to thank ye all fur yer swift attendance. Each of ye here, wi' the exception of oor guests and younger locals, are members of the Loch Ness Preservation Society and has a right, under oor rules, tae speak an' air yer views on the proceedings that occurred today on board the Matthew James. I'll start by asking Jimmy McDermott tae describe what happened." He indicated for James to rise before sitting down himself.

James felt himself colour slightly at the unexpected request as everybody's attention turned to him. He took a deep breath and expertly relayed the details of the day, without pausing, despite the gasps when he mentioned the gun. Finishing, he sat and sipped his coffee, relieved everyone's focus had shifted.

The chairman addressed Matt, asking if he corroborated the story that James had told.

"Absolutely!" said Matt.

Marty also confirmed the sequence of events.

Ryan and Heart said nothing, but listened intently to everything said. Heart was then asked to explain his actions to the assembled group.

"I will not answer questions from a group of vigilantes. This is not your concern, and you should mind your own business this doesn't concern you."

A red-haired, middle-aged policeman stood up and addressed the handcuffed men. "It would be in your best interests to answer the questions put to you here, unless you'd rather be arrested and answer them down at the police station. We could, of course, formally charge you with possession of an illegal firearm and explosive devices, discharging said weapon, causing explosions and threatening behaviour, to name but a few."

Ryan stood up and asked to speak to the chairman away for the members of the public; a wish that was granted, on the condition that two of the police officers accompanied them.

James, Matt and Marty were excused from the rest of the proceedings and trooped into the kitchen to refill their mugs and hunt out the biscuits, whilst Heart was escorted into another small room and watched by one of the other policemen. This left only the members of the Preservation Society in the bar, who immediately started discussing everything that had happened.

Colonel Murray spoke with John Ryan and the members of the constabulary for about half an hour before, apparently satisfied, he addressed the group as a whole again. The doors closed on the bar as he repeated the proposal that Ryan had made, to get their considered opinions.

Sometime later, Maggie came to fetch James and Matt, asking Marty if he would like to join them too. Back in the bar, people were still sitting in the same places, and Ryan and Heart had returned to the room.

The chairman called for attention and waited patiently for the various conversations to finish.

"Ma friends, the events that have taken place today are best described as disgraceful! There is nae guessing what might have happened but for the brave actions of James here and Mr Jackson.

"However, Mr Ryan has made us an offer of compensation as a display of his genuine remorse for the unfortunate incidents, and it is the decision of the group that his offer be accepted as it greatly benefits the local community. In accepting this offer, a strict code of conduct has been placed upon him, with the threat of very serious charges being levelled against him if he errs from his side of the arrangement.

"In the case of Mr Heart, there are to be nae such deals made, and from the moment this meeting is over, he will be driven tae the airport by our friends in the police force, and will return tae the USA on the first available flight. In this community, Mr Heart, we call the shots, not you! If we are all agreed, I'd like tae see a show of hands supporting our decision."

Every member of the congregated group raised their hand, except Matt, James and Marty. James, in particular, couldn't believe what he had just heard, but a look from Maggie prevented him from speaking.

With that, the meeting ended and Heart was led away by the three policemen whilst John Ryan returned to his room.

Chapter 12:
Decisions and Invitations

Seeing that he was unhappy with the majority decision, Maggie indicated to James that he should follow her into the kitchen, where he sat down at the table with Matt by his side. Maggie and Colonel Murray sat down opposite them.

The Colonel started speaking. "The look on yer face tells me ye're no particularly happy with the outcome o' today's events. Tae be honest, I cannae blame ye, fur at face value, Heart appears to have got away wi' his actions without serious consequences. I have tae tell ye though, that more has happened than ye already know.

"So, let's start with Heart. First, he has been sent home with no future option o' returnin' to the United Kingdom. A 'pendin'' file will be created, statin' that he is wanted fur questionin' o'er today's events. If he tries tae return to oor country, no that he would e'er be granted a visa, charges will be brought against him. He has lost his job working for Ryan and will no be paid fur the work that he has completed since he's been here. I agree he's escaped lightly, but other factors were considered that, perhaps, ye're no aware of. Ah'm a great believer in making compromises, ye can often achieve more than expected."

James stayed quiet but reckoned the Colonel was behind this. He decided just to listen.

"The communities aroun' the loch are, in the main, small and fairly isolated. Durin' the past two decades, the young have been leavin' the area in droves tae seek work and futures, an' I cannae blame them. Work aroun' here is scarce and anybody who stays is goin' tae struggle. An' yet, our great hope fur the future is the legend of the Loch Ness Monster. This, more than anythin', is the immediate salvation for oor communities. Why? Because it brings people like Ryan tae oor loch, and tourism, and these bring work and much-needed revenue.

"Ye could argue that we dinnae need types like Ryan but, in simple truth, we do. His investment is invaluable an' the advertisin' an' promotion o' the loch after his findings are published will be priceless to keepin' us on the map an' makin' this a desirable place to visit. If this means that we have tae turn a blind eye tae some o' the more undesirable elements, then it's but a small price tae pay."

Matt nodded, understanding the simple logic, but James hadn't quite lost the anger he was feeling towards both Ryan and Heart. Appearing impassive, he was, in fact, struggling not to allow his conflicting emotions to betray themselves on his face.

"This might sound like a strange question, boys, but I want tae know if ye believe in Nessie, or more accurately, do ye believe in the existence o' Nessie?" the Colonel asked.

Matt looked surprised at the question but thought about it carefully before answering.

"History has produced too many accounts of sightings to dismiss their validity. The sonar evidence suggests something large inhabits the loch with apparent intelligence; it chose to follow us, even adjusting its speed when we did. The equipment doesn't lie; there certainly is something down there. Lorna and Lucy saw something large swimming in the loch, and Pete even caught it on camera. I trust those girls more than anybody alive, except James and Maggie of course, so I'm sure that there is a creature of some sort living in the loch. It doesn't matter whether you call it Nessie or any other name, the creature lives."

The Colonel nodded with apparent pleasure that Matt thought as he did, before focusing his attentive gaze on James.

"And ye, James? Do ye believe in Nessie?"

"My thoughts are identical, something large swims in Ness. Before Ryan, I just accepted the possibility of Nessie's existence, but now I genuinely believe a creature lives in the loch."

"Guid, because that makes wha' I'm aboot to tell ye easier to digest," the Colonel added.

"The society we talked aboot at the earlier meetin' has been runnin' for over twenty years noo, and was started by ma'self and Maggie. Every member, withoot exception, firmly believes in Nessie existing and has, on at least one occasion, witnessed a sightin' at some in point their lives. In total, 126 members make up the society, their sole purpose tae preserve the way o' life here in the communities.

"More recently, it has been devoted to keepin' the communities goin'. I've already said aboot the young leavin' in droves tae seek a better life, but it is the young we need tae keep most tae ensure future generations here. People like yerselves and the twins who love the loch an' its peaceful communities. Durin' the past ten years, many properties aroun' the loch, have been left uninhabited and unsold because o' the lack o' work an' the society has bought them up cheaply. It's oor intention tae offer them tae the young, local people who can manage tae get enough work tae enable them tae stay. The only stipulations bein' that they must believe in Nessie, become members o' the society an', if they e'er leave, forfeit their right tae the accommodation. They will also have tae maintain the secrecy of oor society."

The Colonel held a captive audience, in his element as a

81

charismatic speaker and organiser.

"No 300 yards away fae where yoor boat is moored, are two semi-detached stone cottages that belong tae the society. The stonework is structurally sound, but they need new roofs, some dryin'-oot an' a spot of modernisation. Ryan has agreed tae fut the entire bill fur their repair an' three others as well. He's an extremely wealthy man an' this expense is a drop in the ocean tae him. Ye can call it compensation if ye like, or e'en an attempt at bribery, but it benefits our community, and tha's what matters tae us most. It is ma wish that you two manage two cottages near yer moorin's where ye can continue to work an' live as part o' the community. No finer young men exist in this community than you. Ye work hard, support others an' scratch oot a meagre existence here, an' appear tae be completely satisfied with the life. We want ye tae stay an', let's be honest, ye cannae live on that boat forever noo, can ye?" The Colonel finished his rhetoric, and waited patiently for a reply.

Both Matt and James remained quiet, aware of the seriousness of the decision they were making.

Matt responded first. "Will we have to cook our own venison stew?"

The Colonel appeared confused at the question, but Maggie answered.

"Ye've been and always will be welcome tae join me fur yer evenin' meal after a hard day's work, but if ye're no working, then I expect tae be invited tae yers fur the same," she said, laughing.

"Are we in agreement?" asked the Colonel, a little confused.

"That means, sir, that you have two enormous yeses'," James told him and reached out to shake the Colonel's hand.

The Colonel informed them that work on the cottages would start this week and announced his departure.

The rest of the secret society members had left soon after the meeting, and Maggie now started to sort out dinner for her remaining guests and the boys. They kept her company for a while, asking about the latest news on Lorna. She told them she would be home in the morning, admitting how relieved she was that the injuries weren't more severe than they were, and said that she would oversee Lorna's recovery herself.

The boys couldn't wait to share their news with the twins, James in particular, wanted to check on Lorna himself. He didn't wait long before Lucy arrived in the kitchen with Pete, her face tired and drawn.

She sat down heavily at the table, sipping gratefully at the mug of tea that Maggie quickly placed in front of her. "A dreadful day!" she said with a wan smile.

"Aye, bairn, ye must have been worried sick aboot that poor sister o' yours. But there's more tae tell, I'm afraid…"

Lucy looked up, raising her eyebrows with interest as the boys started to share the day's adventures.

The following morning, Pete got up early and head back to the hospital to bring Lorna home as soon as she was discharged.

Lucy had slept in late, after a fitful night, but was downstairs finishing breakfast when Pete returned, carrying Lorna in his arms.

"Where would you like the invalid, Maggie?" he asked, jovially.

"I want the sitting room where I can meet and greet everybody. I'll not be confined to my room," she said quickly, before Maggie suggested otherwise.

"My goodness she sounds like you, Lucy told Maggie with a grin.

"I suppose that livin' wi' me all these years has made ye girls as headstrong as me!" said Maggie with a sigh of mock horror.

"I'd better make up a nest fur ye then!"

With the excitement of yesterday over, Nessie hunting was temporarily suspended. Ryan remained closeted in his room all day, apparently "doing research", but Marty and Pete joined the others downstairs where they passed the time playing cards and board games, reassured that Lorna was well enough to partake.

The following day only Lucy and Pete went out to collect films. Marty had gone to check the sonar device. He said that as the equipment was highly sensitive, he was concerned it may have suffered damage after the depth-charge incident.

Matt and James were leaving for the boat after briefly checking in on Lorna, when interrupted by a surprise visit from Colonel Murray. He wanted to make arrangements to show them the properties earmarked for them. James suspected the Colonel wanted to discuss more, as he accompanied them to the boat.

Marty was squatting down on the deck with the inner workings of the sonar device arrayed in front of him.

"Good afternoon, Marty," the Colonel greeted him, shaking his hand amiably. "I hoped I would come across ye today as I didnae get a chance tae thank ye fur yer part in disarming Heart the other day."

"It was nothing, Colonel. Heart is an unpleasant individual, the expedition will improve for his absence," Marty replied, warmly.

"There is somethin' else that I'd like tae discuss with ye an' the boys here, a matter o' some concern tae me an' the society. I do hope ye can spare a few moments of yer time."

"Sure, Colonel. What's on your mind?"

"Ryan is at the centre of ma thoughts right noo, I'm afraid."

Matt suggested that they go down below where they could sit more comfortably. The Colonel didn't seem to mind, despite the difficulty he had negotiating the steep ladder. When they were all seated, he shared some of his concerns.

"Mr Ryan is driven, no doubt contributing to his success, but he makes very dubious decisions. His basic intentions are honourable, but when it comes tae the possibility of increasin' fame an' fortune, I feel he may make the wrong decision again. Tae that point, I believe he poses a real threat tae those around him. He wants tae catch Nessie first an' foremost, an' that goes against the interest o' the locals. We are completely happy fur him tae capture film o' the creature, make sonar contact an' even see her fur himself, but we absolutely cannae allow him tae catch or harm her. I'm also *very* concerned fur yer safety. Ye must watch each other's backs, fur obvious reasons."

He described what the creature meant to the locals, how important Nessie was to their existence on the loch, and the likely happenings if Nessie was captured or removed from the region.

Marty explained to the Colonel how he made his living, and the number of scientific anomalies he had discovered around the world. He showed his pleasure at providing evidence of Nessie, without actually seeing the creature with his own eyes, yet.

The Colonel asked him outright to help ensure Nessie's safety, apologising for not being able to offer any form of remuneration for his efforts. He beamed when Marty replied that occasionally preserving something was payment enough.

After reiterating his thoughts that Ryan could pose further danger, and needed to be watched carefully, the Colonel left.

They watched the Colonel disappear before nodding at each other, the Colonel was correct, Ryan needed watching, and they had just been selected for the task.

A red-haired, middle-aged police officer stood up and addressed the handcuffed men. "It would be in yer best interests to answer the questions put to ye here, unless ye'd rather be arrested and answer them doon at the police station. We could, of course, formally charge you with possession of an illegal firearm and explosive devices, discharging said weapon, causing explosions and threatening behaviour, to name but a few."

Ryan stood and asked to speak to the chairman in private. The wish was granted, on the condition that police officers accompanied them.

James, Matt and Marty were excused from the proceedings and trooped into the kitchen to refill their mugs and hunt out biscuits. Heart was escorted into another room and guarded by a police officer. Only the members of the Preservation Society remained at the bar, who immediately started discussing the events.

Colonel Murray spoke with John Ryan and the members of the constabulary for about half an hour before, apparently satisfied, he addressed the group again. The doors closed on the bar as he repeated the proposal that Ryan had made, to get their considered opinions.

Sometime later, Maggie came to fetch James and Matt, asking Marty if he would like to join them too. In the bar, people had retained their places, as Ryan and Heart were escorted in.

The chairman called for attention and waited patiently for the various conversations to finish.

"Ma friends, the events that have taken place today are best described as disgraceful! The outcome may have been different but fur the brave actions of James and Mr Johnson.

"However, Mr Ryan has made us an offer of compensation as a display of his genuine remorse fur the unfortunate incidents, and it is the decision of the group that his offer be accepted as it greatly benefits the local community. In accepting this offer, a strict code o' conduct has been placed upon him, with the threat of very serious charges being levelled against him if he strays from his side of the arrangement.

"In the case o' Mr Heart, there can be no deals, and the

moment this meeting concludes, he'll be driven tae the airport by the police, returnin' tae the USA on the first available flight. In this community, Mr Heart, we call the shots, not you! If we are all agreed, I'd like tae see a show o' hands supporting oor decision."

Every member of the congregated group raised their hand, except Matt, James and Marty. James couldn't believe the turn of events, but Maggie prevented him from speaking.

With that, the meeting ended and Heart was led away by the three police officers whilst John Ryan returned to his room.

Chapter 13:
Back to Work

The following week continued mundanely, the boys continued sweeping the loch, but without contacting Nessie.

Both Matt and James held concerns the depth charge might have injured her, but Ryan informed they were designed to stun. He stated logically, that with only two days of sonar sweeps remaining, if they had killed the creature, it would appear on the monitor at the bottom of the loch, a point that Marty agreed with.

Lucy and Pete continued with the camera observation work, but neither had recorded any more sightings after their initial success.

With Heart gone, Lorna was acting as Ryan's 'gofer', suggesting she could organise whatever he needed with the telephone, and proved it with a quick turnaround on any of his requests.

Although obviously doing his best to be civil to everyone, nothing could change the fact that Ryan was an unpleasant individual whom few people liked. An element of frustration, caused by the lack of results, was creeping into his persona and he could not hide his discontent from those around him, becoming increasingly impatient and tetchy with little provocation. It was Marty who noticed first, warning that trouble was around the corner.

Ryan was keen to finish the initial sonar mapping so that he could concentrate on the areas he selected as most likely to get sonar hits of Nessie. The filming would continue for the duration of the mission, but he wanted to include four cameras at the water's edge, hoping to capture a close-up image if the creature emerged; at this stage, it meant sacrificing cameras from the higher ground.

On the first morning of the third week, and on the return leg of their first sweep, they achieved sonar contact with the underwater creature, who once again followed their boat down the loch. Ryan ordered small changes of speed and direction to observe the creature's response, and again it mirrored their every move, always staying twenty metres behind the boat.

Ryan gave the order that, once it started to move away, they should try to position the boat behind it, so that they could follow it, but despite James' best efforts, the creature remained glued to their stern.

For forty minutes, the creature followed the boat like a dog on a lead, before suddenly veering away. Marty called the directional change and James responded immediately, keeping it behind them. It changed course several times and each time, the skill of the men kept it on the sonar screen, before it suddenly sped up, speeding past underneath before James had time to move the throttle lever in response.

The boat was soon moving at full throttle and they all watched in disappointment as the creature increased the gap between them and disappeared from the sonar screen completely, free from its pursuers.

"Chase it, chase it! Don't let it get away," shouted Ryan, his anger reappearing. He kicked out at some rope netting, venting some frustration at losing his quarry once again.

"We need a faster boat for the stage two of the operation. We can't have it constantly outpacing us or we'll never discover its secrets," he blazed.

"We have learnt a lot already, though," said James suddenly, to pacify the angry man.

"Just what have we *learnt*?" asked Ryan, sarcastically.

"For a start, we're dealing with an exceptionally intelligent creature, that's evident. She's capable of following our boat, matching our speed and direction at will. When she decides she's had enough, she increases hers to get away. When we match her speed, she speeds up again and then, almost in defiance, demonstrates she can leave us in her wake. It's almost like a child playing a game.

"We've seen that the sonar readings have all occurred at the southern end of the loch. And I've also noticed that this same area of the loch holds the highest amount of fish stocks. Since we can assume that she feeds on fish, I would suggest that this is probably the best area of the loch for her to live, and thus, where we should focus in our search."

Ryan's anger gradually subsided as he listened attentively to James' conclusions.

"You're quite right in your assertions, and when we've finally finished mapping the bottom of the loch, this is where we'll concentrate our efforts. But we'll definitely need a faster boat for that stage of the mission, I'll get Lorna onto that tonight. The sooner we have that, the greater the likelihood of success. Ok, let's finish the sweep we were on. That'll be another step closer to the second stage."

Marty gave James the thumbs up behind Ryan's back and they all returned to their tasks.

At the evening meeting, Ryan took his time for once as he set out his plans for the forthcoming second stage of operations.

"The sooner the sonar mapping is completed, the better. I wonder if it's possible to work a night shift tomorrow to conclude this quickly. If calculations are accurate, we would finish before dawn, if starting at seven. Since you're the main pilot, Matt, what do you think?"

"It's possible, although keeping the boat on a true course at night will be more challenging without visual points of reference, but it can be done by compass alone," Matt told him.

"If so, we can start later the following day, about ten o'clock. That will be different! Lorna, I want you to organise a faster boat for us. There are others on the loch, similarly sized, but with a greater top speed. The idea is to sweep across the loch at the southern end. The recent sightings originate there. When sonar contact is made, I want to follow Nessie for as long as possible, collecting data about its capabilities. Pete, can you organise some underwater cameras that can be towed behind the boat?"

"I can, but we'd need a very strong light source as there's little natural light at the depth Nessie seems to frequent. We'd also need some sort of remote-control system, or the light may just stop her from making an appearance. This could take several days to organise and set up."

"You can have two days. Don't worry about expense, tell Lorna what you need and she'll organize it."

Ryan continued with his seemingly endless list of demands. "Right, move the cameras from the northern end to here; I want pictures from above and at water level. How long will that take?"

"The same, two days, possibly longer. Working on those means I can't be work on the underwater equipment."

"Fair enough, but work late if necessary. Our sponsors have only given us a maximum of four weeks and the third has already started," he concluded.

Pete looked up suddenly. "If we're going to chase this

creature across the loch at speed, the underwater camera will lift and may miss its target. It'll need weighing down."

Marty made a suggestion. "I noticed the boat has a massive anchor, one of those old-fashioned iron ones. Mark off eighty feet on the chain and attach the camera to that."

"Even that will rise if we travel at speed. I would set the camera at the sixty-foot point and then mark off the rest of the anchor chain in increments of five feet. That should give us a pretty good chance of matching Nessie's depth in the water," James suggested.

For once, Ryan appeared content with their progress and the positive contributions from the team.

"Sounds like we have a plan! My final suggestion is that we eat well and retire early, tomorrow will be a mighty long day."

Matt and James went into the kitchen to report the plans to Maggie. She looked at them with concern in her eyes.

"I still think he's up tae somethin'. He's trying too hard tae be nice tae everyone an', in ma experience, tha's no his normal way. I still believe he's going tae try an' capture Nessie an' we cannae let that happen. Even if he disnae manage it, he may well harm her in his efforts."

"There's no way we're going to let that happen, Maggie, I promise you. We understand the importance of this animal and what it means to the community. We'll protect it at all costs," said James, trying to reassure her.

"I know ye will, laddie, but Ryan is used to getting his own way an' will stop at nothin' tae get what he wants."

"He faces a significant force, the loch people won't accept this happening," interjected Matt.

"I just hope ye're right, pet."

The boys left her with Lorna who had spent long periods alone during the week.

As soon as they'd gone, Maggie went to the telephone and

called Colonel Murray, voicing her concerns to her old friend. He reassured her the people could be called upon and would respond in numbers if required.

Everything went to plan the next day. The sweeps ended sooner than anticipated, and Lucy and Pete completed the moving of the cameras, setting off at dawn to utilise all the daylight hours.

Lorna contacted the owner of the most powerful vessel on the loch, capable of nearly twice the speed of the Matthew James, and he agreed to bring it down early the following morning. Marty, Matt and James were to transfer their equipment to the new boat, while Lucy helped Pete start work on the underwater equipment that Lorna had located and had delivered by special courier.

James was impressed at Lorna's speed and commented to Matt how efficient she was, especially with no internet at her disposal.

Thankfully, Ryan kept himself scarce, appearing just once during the day to check on everybody's progress, congratulating them on their efforts.

'Maggie's right, he's being *too* nice,' thought Matt, making it a personal mission to keep a close eye on him during the next stage.

Chapter 14:
On Nessie's Tail

The new boat was modern and sleek, making the Matthew James seem quite old-fashioned when it first appeared. Matt and James shared the wheel, gaining a feel for the new controls and discovering how the strange boat responded. Both, were soon as comfortable with the Katie Marie as their own boat. They found her quick to accelerate with her powerful engine and loved the way she turned almost on a sixpence.

The camera equipment was attached to the anchor from the Matthew James, larger and heavier than the Katie Marie's. Everything was prepared and the daily sweeps continued, backwards and forwards across the width of the loch.

On the second day, they saw Nessie reappear on the sonar. Marty called to Ryan who was out on deck inspecting the underwater camera equipment. Ryan gave the order for the anchor, complete with the camera and light attachments, to be lowered to a depth of seventy feet.

As soon as it was in position, Pete took the seat next to Marty and switched it on, gluing his eyes to the monitor. The two of them sat motionless, without blinking, as they watched and waited.

"Nessie is right behind us, matching our course and speed," Marty announced.

"No visual sighting, as yet," Pete called out and asked Matt to lower the camera another five feet.

"Contact still maintaining course and speed," said Marty a moment later.

"Another five feet please, Matt," said Pete. Matt duly complied.

Suddenly Pete called out excitedly. "There she is, gentlemen! Let me introduce you to Nessie!"

On the camera monitor, a dark shape appeared just below and in front of the camera. They all stared, unable to discern detail in the gloomy depths of the loch, even with the artificial light source.

"We need a better image," said Ryan, frustrated at being unable to see clearer. "I mean, what the hell are we looking at here?"

"Look carefully, see the tail, making sideway sweeps? You can also see the rest of the body. Look there, two rear limbs or fins descending in front of the tail," Pete told them.

James understood what Pete described before becoming distracted by the tail flashing across the screen.

"I can see it too," he exclaimed in excitement.

Ryan nodded, before picking up his rucksack and taking out a sheaf of papers. He quickly rifled through them and placed a single sheet on the table.

They looked at the image of a plesiosaur.

"Compare with the screen image and tell me your conclusions," Ryan commanded.

There's no doubt about the similarity, if not a positive match, to the picture on the table.

"It looks the same, but without seeing the anterior view, I

can't verify that," Pete told him.

"Let's try to gain a frontal view, then. Matt, increase speed! Pete, rotate the camera one hundred and eighty degrees!"

Both reacted immediately, and the creature temporarily disappeared from view.

"She's sped up as well," Marty shouted.

"Increase speed again, Matt!" shouted Ryan in exasperation.

Matt turned the throttle, and the boat picked up another few knots of speed.

"She's still keeping pace with us," Marty responded, so Matt pushed the throttle again without waiting for the order.

Then, without warning, their quarry altered course. Marty bellowed out the direction and Matt responded at the helm; but making the turn depleted the speed of the boat.

"It's right on the edge of the sonar range, more speed or we'll lose it!"

Matt opened the throttle to maximum and the boat almost lurched as the propeller frantically increased its revolutions.

Slowly, the boat gained on the plesiosaur until it appeared central on the sonar screen. However, still nothing showed on the camera.

"The extra speed is making the camera rise. Try lowering it another five feet," suggested Pete.

James dashed outside to deal with it, then raced back to the wheelhouse.

"Creature turning starboard, twenty degrees," called Marty.

Matt made the correction. The boat leaned into the turn, but its speed bled away.

The animal suddenly turned again, disappearing off the sonar screen completely. Ryan ordered Matt to move in a zigzag search pattern to try to pick up the signal again, but it was all in vain and, despite the manoeuvres, Nessie did not reappear.

They continued to zigzag for a further half hour before he pulled back the throttle lever and brought the boat to a standstill.

Ryan thumped the table with his fist. "We were so close, so close!" he said in complete and utter frustration. "That thing moves like lightning and this boat isn't fast enough, either. Marty, can you increase the width of the sonar scan to allow us to contact the creature earlier?"

"It's possible to adjust the angle of the sweep, but the modifications would be time-consuming," Marty told him.

"How long?"

"If I start now, I might just finish the work late tonight. But the adjustments could mess up the readings, especially as the instruments are already set for optimal performance."

"We must keep it in our sights long enough to film it. Pete, I want you to increase the lighting down there. We need more detail, do whatever it takes! Matt, take us home so that we can start on the modifications," Ryan ordered.

Matt turned the boat towards home as James and Pete raised the trailing anchor a few feet at a time. This required a delicate touch to avoid it tangling with, and damaging the sonar cables, so Marty decided to retrieve the sonar simultaneously, minimising the risk. Running at a shallower depth than the anchor, it should rise quickly and clear of the chain.

The first cable appeared untangled, and Ryan worked with Marty to haul it aboard. The anchor followed a few minutes later, and Pete disconnected the camera and light. Both men decided to carry out the delicate adjustments at Maggie's. Pete had already decided to try a wider lens on the camera to compensate for Nessie's massive size.

Before long, they were back at the boarding house asking Maggie if she objected to them working in the spacious lounge-dining area.

Given the go-ahead, the equipment was brought in and laid neatly on newspapers, to avoid damaging the table surfaces.

Lucy worked with Pete, discovering that the more time she spent with him, the more her fascination with photography increased. She was keen to learn everything from this very accomplished photographer.

Marty was different; the sonar device was his baby, and he required time alone to achieve his objectives. Disappearing to his room, Ryan left the boys with spare time. They were just discussing a visit to the cottages to see how the repairs were progressing, when he re-appeared requesting their attention.

He unfolded the large map of the loch with the sonar sweep lines marked on it. Laying it on a table, he weighed down the four corners before speaking.

"I know you've seen this map before, but I thought it would help to see all the points where the sonar located Nessie. This is Nessie's first sounding location, this, where she disappeared."

He drew a line on the map between the two points. Then he drew more lines in similar fashion to mark other sonar soundings.

As the four lines formed a rough, unconnected trapezium, Matt and James realised immediately what he was surmising.

Ryan joined them with dashed lines. In terms of the entire loch, the shape covered a tiny part of it.

"It would seem that this area is very important to our plesiosaur and I would suggest that it forms its 'home range'. Although I don't want to put all my eggs in one basket, so to speak, I think we should concentrate our search within that area. If we cannot make contact, we'll just widen the area on all four sides until we do.

"Hopefully, with a wider sonar sweeping area, we'll save an enormous amount of time by making fewer sweeps. What do you think?"

"It's a good idea and one that will pay dividends, as long as

Nessie plays ball! But so far, she always seems to be one step ahead of us. This animal is definitely intelligent! One thing occurs to me, what if there's more than one?"

"No one's mentioned that, James, but I've been thinking the same thing. I'm actually wondering if the creature has young to protect. That would give it good reason to stay in a confined area in such a large loch," Ryan finished.

"I'd like to transfer the coordinates of that area onto the chart in the boat before we set out tomorrow," said Matt.

Ryan nodded and rolled up his map, then left without another word.

For the rest of the day, Lucy worked with Pete Jackson, who suggested she joined him as his assistant on the boat the following day. He was delighted at having her help as well as her company, relishing the opportunity of teaching someone as passionate about photography as he was.

Poor Lorna felt disappointed, unable to go despite hobbling around with the crutch's aid. The tasks Ryan gave her were completed quickly and with little to occupy her she felt quite bored and isolated. Although she didn't fuss, Matt and James noticed how much quieter she had become, correctly surmising the reason, and decided to visit to the cottages, now in the process of renovation. She beamed at their thoughtfulness.

Maggie made a surprise appearance as they left and insisted on driving them to the cottages. "Yer hand will be raw with blisters, walkin' with that, she told her adopted daughter.

Lorna smiled, gratefully; her day improving by the minute.

At the cottages, Matt and James were surprised and impressed at the speed of refurbishments. The roof was dismantled, and fresh trusses installed, the old plaster covering the stone walls stripped away, and the upstairs flooring completely removed, allowing a view of the sky from the downstairs spaces.

"These are going to be just lovely when they're finished, Jimmy. You'll need a woman to share with," Lorna smiled with a sideways glance.

James realised the implication of what she was saying and took a playful approach.

"Another woman, Maggie meets my every need?"

Lorna slapped him hard on the shoulder whilst Matt laughed out loud.

"It's no good you laughing, Matthew. Just wait till I tell Lucy about this!"

Matt adopted a mock look of fear and received a slap as well.

"Dinnae worry, Lorna. They'll soon change their minds when I tell them I'm getting far too old tae take care o' them for much longer," Maggie told her.

"In that case, Maggie, we'll have to move in and take care of you instead!" James told her.

"Och no, ye're nae. It's bad enough having ye roond tae dinner most nights, withoot having ye under ma feet all day, as well!" she retorted, looking horrified at the very idea.

Chapter 15:
Nessie Surfaces

They returned to the water the next day, zigzagging the area Ryan plotted previously. On their third sweep, the sonar detected Nessie once again. She took up a familiar place behind the boat, about seventy feet below them.

"Lower the anchor chain!" directed Ryan immediately, and it was dropped to a depth of eighty feet to compensate for the uplift as it trailed behind them.

The camera collected the image of Nessie but, with the increased light, a dark-green hue to its colouring became evident.

"Increase speed by five knots!"

Matt pushed forward the throttle lever. Nessie followed suit, matching their speed perfectly and staying in position behind them.

"Another five knots!" Ryan called out.

The boat raced forward, gradually gaining pace. They continued for ten minutes, gradually increasing the speed until, as yesterday, they were travelling at the Katy Marie's top speed. Still, Nessie followed, seemingly effortlessly, and Ryan thumped the table in vexation when he realised that the boat could go no faster.

"Prepare to follow when she veers off. I don't think she can sustain these speeds for long without tiring. With a bit of luck, we might track her to where she hides," Ryan said, still thinking tactically, even in the turmoil of his frustration.

After ten minutes, the creature began to veer off and Marty immediately called out the bearing. Matt's response was instantaneous, and the boat turned a full ninety degrees, making it list alarmingly. Unlike yesterday, however, they kept Nessie on the sonar screen. Unfortunately, the underwater camera was rendered useless as they followed Nessie, instead it following them.

As Pete and Lucy went to the stern to retrieve the camera equipment, Marty called a drop in the creature's speed as it altered course once more. Matt pulled back slightly on the throttle to match the beast's speed; Ryan's guess that it was tiring seemed to hold true.

It turned abruptly several times; each a fraction slower than the previous before Marty announced it head towards the surface. Everybody went on deck in anticipation of a sighting, except Matt and Marty whose concentration on their task was absolute.

"Thirty feet," Marty called out. "Twenty… Ten! Surfacing starboard side of the boat," he yelled.

Everybody's eyes became glued to the water. At first, nothing was apparent, but as the creature ascended, the water above rose before the hump of the creature's back broke the surface and dispersed it. Pete acted immediately, grabbing a couple of cameras and giving one to Lucy.

"Take as many as you can," he told her excitedly.

The creature was swimming much more slowly now, and Matt pulled back the throttle lever to match the slower pace and keep Nessie alongside. The visible part of it, above the water, showed green- grey, mottled, scaly skin, but there was no sign of its head or the long neck that would enable the scientists to confirm its identity as a plesiosaur.

102

As they watched, a tail gently extended out of the water. Nobody said a word, staring in anticipation and wonder; a sight few were fortunate to witness. Suddenly, Nessie raised her long tail high into the air and beat it down hard on the surface. Gallons of water were sent shooting into the air to plunge down coldly onto the assembled observers with a loud splash. The creature repeated this move, flooding the deck and its occupants once more.

Fearing for the film inside, Pete and Lucy stopped clicking the camera shutters and dashed into the wheelhouse as, then with a final thrashing of its tail, Nessie slipped silently beneath the loch.

With Ryan shouting the order to pursue, Marty called out the bearing and Matt hurriedly turned the wheel, but this time the creature did not offer a challenge, maintaining a steady speed and straight direction. The boat followed for three miles, travelling north, before its quarry made a final turn and simply disappeared from the sonar screen.

"What happened? Where did it go?" exclaimed Ryan in disappointment.

"I don't know. One second it was here and the next It was gone!" offered a bemused Marty. "Somewhere between us and the shoreline, thirty yards away. The equipment's fine, everything checks out, so I'm at a loss why we're no longer receiving a signal."

Ryan didn't respond to this, instead simply giving the order to head back to base.

"I want those pictures developed as soon as we get back, Pete, and I want them brought to the meeting at six tonight. Marty, I suggest you do some thorough checks on the sonar, the creature can't simply disappear. Take us home, Matt, so we can all get some dry clothes and some strong coffee."

Knowing that there was nothing wrong with his equipment, a thought struck Marty that might explain Nessie's sudden disappearance and he asked James if he would like to help him complete his sonar chart that afternoon. James was pleased to partake in the proceedings, since Matt dominated the piloting of the new boat.

Pleased that her interest in photography, was so keen, Pete offered to show Lucy how to develop the pictures they had taken and was delighted when she took him up on the idea. Despite realising the films required time for developing, Ryan carried no doubts that Nessie was a plesiosaur. He would win fame and fortune for discovering a living creature from the dinosaur age. He hoped that the photographs taken would prove his conclusions beyond any doubt.

After the others had parted, James boarded his own boat to change, before returning to the wheelhouse. Marty waited patiently for him.

"What's up Marty? I felt you knew more but sharing it wasn't an option."

"You're right, and I thought I had everything I needed to prove it. Unfortunately, I don't. I need to return to the guesthouse to check some readings from last week."

"Will you share now or make me wait till later?"

"Nessie didn't disappear, she just went home," said Marty with a tantalising grin. "You've got to see what I've found!"

Briskly, they walked back, making their way straight to Marty's room, seeing no one. Once there, Marty found a copy of the map that Ryan used and laid a thin sheet of clear plastic on top. On it were marked the same sweep lines, but he'd added depth and distance measurements too.

"Look at this area. It's slightly north of where we usually find Nessie appearing on sonar, and it's the area she disappeared in today. See the distance measurements here and here." He stabbed the map with his forefinger. "The sonar says that the distance across the loch is this, but in actual yardage, it's less. The figures don't match; in fact, they're exactly twelve yards out. The sonar recorded twelve yards more of water than the map shows, only one explanation for that."

James waited expectantly for him to continue, but Marty was revelling in his solution of the apparent anomaly.

He paused briefly, before speaking with rising excitement.

"The twelve-yard difference is *underwater*. It's either an underwater cave or a large overhang beneath the water. The shore at this point is pretty non-existent because there's a steep incline that starts from within the loch, if you like a sort of cliff; and it's under this cliff that I reckon Nessie lives."

James nodded in understanding. "So why not tell Ryan?"

"I'm worried he'd try to catch her, and stop at nothing to do it, even if it means killing the creature. Half the beauty of what I do for a living is proving the existence of something and seeing it filmed it in its natural environment without harming it. Loch Ness is famous for its mystery and I don't want to change that. Remove Nessie and, no more mystery. Why else would people come?"

"You're absolutely right, Marty. Nessie is the main attraction for visiting. Without the myth, local people would lose their employment and forced to leave. I, for one, am glad you didn't tell Ryan."

"Hopefully, the underwater shots and sonar contacts, along with Pete and Lucy's pictures will be enough and he'll leave here satisfied," Marty concluded.

Suddenly, a noise outside the room interrupted them, and James gave Marty an ominous look. Marty opened the door. There was nobody there but a solitary piece of paper lying on the floor. The paper was blank except for a printed address at the top with Ryan's name above it. They closed the door quietly.

"He was outside listening to us!" James whispered.

Marty shrugged his shoulders. "It certainly seems so."

James explained the recent events to Matt and Maggie.

"I think oor Mr Ryan needs tae be watched carefully for the rest o' his time here. I agree with Marty an' the Colonel that this man is capable of anything, an' I don't intend tae see any harm coming tae Nessie. So far, all he's done is prove what many o' we locals already knew, so it's no matter if he shows his evidence tae the world. Ach, what's important here is that Nessie stays in the loch, continuing tae attract the tourists that support our community.

"I'll report this tae the Colonel an' the rest of the group. He'll ken what tae do for the best; he always does," Maggie decided. "Tonight's briefing is going tae be interesting. Ryan has tae show his next move so I want ye tae listen carefully tae what he says, and tae what he *disnae* say. Put yersel' in his shoes, what'd ye do next? If it disnae match with what he says, it'll be because he's up tae somethin'."

"I'll pay attention, Maggie, very close attention, I can promise you that," said James.

Chapter 16:
Strange Happenings

John Ryan, standing outside Marty's room the whole time, had heard every word that Marty said. From the detail of Marty's explanation, he knew that he would be able pinpoint Nessie's secret lair, and his thoughts were already filled with capturing her. He crept back to his room and shut the door, unaware a sheet of paper from the bundle he carried had fallen silently to the floor.

Quickly spreading his map of the loch on the bed, he scanned the rough location that he'd heard described. Within seconds, he had pinpointed the place where cliffs rose from the loch, showing the locale of the loch monster's lair. Already, putting together a plan; a ruthless plan, one to secure his fame and fortune forever as 'The man who caught Nessie'. The very thought sent shivers of excitement coursing through his body.

Needing to make several phone calls, where he wouldn't be overheard, Ryan grabbed his jacket and left the boarding house, walking to the s i n g l e public telephone box in the village. He ran out of change halfway through his list of calls, so walked the short distance to the village shop to replenish his supply, before continuing. Once he'd finally put down the receiver in the stuffy kiosk, he went back to Maggie's to prepare for the evening meeting.

At six o'clock, everybody assembled in the lounge area, waiting for Ryan to make his daily appearance, unaccustomed to finding this meticulous man running late.

The mood in the room was uneasy; some muttered in low voices, glancing furtively towards the door, aware Ryan could stride in arrogantly at any moment.

James and Matt had realised something was amiss, the great net could have been used on Nessie when she was swimming alongside the boat, and her capture secured whilst weakened after the chase. They had discussed this at length, knowing that Ryan was not one to waste an opportunity. It just made little sense.

Ten minutes later than usual, Ryan made his appearance, apologising for his tardiness before thanking everyone for attending.

"The number of days left of the expedition are depleting fast, it's time to prepare for the final stage of our mission. All our remaining efforts are to be focused on encouraging Nessie to surface so we can film it close up.

"Tomorrow I want Pete and Lucy to retrieve all the cameras positioned around the loch and check the footage for any evidence caught on film. Since the images obtained from the boat are superior, the need for further investment, in terms of man-power and finances on fixed location photography is pointless.

"Pete, I'd like you to organise any equipment that might benefit the filming of Nessie from the boat. Buy the best on the market, because you realise, when this goes public, the sceptics will endeavour to prove the images are either inconclusive or faked.

"Matt and Jimmy, I will arrange for some of the equipment on board the boat to be removed tomorrow, increasing the amount of available work space, and allowing additional room for tripods and cameras. As such, we'll not be venturing onto the loch at all. Apart from our preparations, I think it most unlikely that the animal will show up. It was clearly tired the way we pushed it today, so it would be prudent to allow it to rest for the day.

"Marty, the use of the sonar is clearly paramount; I want you to check everything thoroughly and prepare for the next sortie. We're so close now to having all the proof we'll ever need, that we can't take the risk of equipment failure.

"Now Pete, I've decided not to use the underwater camera and lighting. The pictures we've captured, to date, have not provided sufficient detail, and I don't want to stretch you in different directions, and risk losing quality film footage because of it.

"Any other thoughts, people?" finished Ryan, waiting expectantly for someone to speak up. Nobody did, so he left the room as briskly as he'd entered it.

The boys glanced at Maggie and raised their eyebrows, suggesting a discussion was required. They sauntered out to the kitchen.

"What's up, boys? Is somethin' botherin' ye?" asked Maggie as soon as they had sat down.

"Something's not quite right, Maggie. In fact, *nothing* is right," answered Matt in a worried tone.

James joined in. "First and importantly, there are three days remaining of Ryan's expedition. If I were him, I wouldn't waste a day on needless preparations. I'd be on the lock. Second, he said it himself, all the film footage will be scrutinised intensely, so why remove any camera that might just provide the proof of Nessie's existence? Third, that rubbish he spouted about giving Nessie time to recover! I wouldn't want to miss an opportunity of following Nessie in a weakened state because, when she's fully fit, we don't have a hope of matching her speed and agility so have next to no chance of success."

Matt spoke again. "It's almost like he's playing for time. The tasks he's given us are meaningless. The sonar doesn't need servicing; it's been completely reliable, and Marty checks it every day, anyway. There's plenty of space on the hired boat for any amount of equipment, so this is either to keep us busy, or more likely, away from them, I'm absolutely convinced."

"I think ye're right. He's clearly playin' fur time here, an' the question has tae be why? If he wants us oot o' the way fur a while, it's because somethin' *else* is goin' tae happen here that, clearly, he disnae want us involved with. I think he still wants to catch Nessie. I've said it afore and I'll say it again; he *knows* that we'd no allow it, so has improvised an alternate plan that nae includes us. If this is the case, then it's goin' tae happen at night. He could'nae get away wi' it in broad daylight. This gives him two opportunities; either tonight or tomorrow night and ma guess is that it'll be on the morrow. Tonight, is too soon, and he's no goin' tae be able tae accomplish this without help. He's goin' tae need plenty, considerable manpower. If anyone new arrived aroun' here, I'd have heard, so I expect them to appear sometime on the morrow," expounded Maggie.

"Not necessarily, Maggie, strangers here raise questions awkward to answer. I reckon they'd arrive quietly, keeping out of sight somewhere," suggested James.

"I'm goin' tae contact the Colonel an' tell him what we suspect. I'm sure that he can organise a string o' lookouts at suitable locations where they might turn up," Maggie told them.

The sun had descended below the horizon before the boys returned to their boat, but the night was beautifully clear. Stars sparkled in their millions and a brilliant full moon illuminated their path with a silvery glow.

They walked in silence, each lost in his own thoughts and fears for the anticipated showdown. Neither wished to disturb the quiet companionship borne from a lifetime of shared experiences.

As they boarded the Matthew James, the moonlight reflected on the shimmering loch towards them, creating the illusion of an ice shelf on the motionless water. They stopped to admire its beauty before descending below deck to make preparations for the night's sleep.

Laying in their bunks, only half-aware of the distant hoot of an owl, they drifted to sleep at the gentle, rhythmic lapping of the water against the side of their boat.

Shortly after three in the morning, Matt awoke suddenly and lay blinking his eyes, feeling a prickle of apprehension and wondering what was amiss. Except for James' peaceful breathing in the opposite bunk, he discerned no other sound. Something had disturbed his sleep though, to the degree that he was now completely awake and alert. There came a sound, clear and distinct. Footsteps; not on this boat, but the hired one moored alongside.

Slipping out of his bunk, Matt gently shook James awake, placing his hand lightly across his mouth to prevent him from speaking. James woke with a start, but it took several seconds staring at Matt with wide, dream-filled eyes for him to realise what was happening.

"We have visitors!" Matt whispered as he released his hand from James' mouth and allowed him to slip from his bunk. "Get dressed quickly."

As soon as they were ready, they crept stealthily up the steep steps to the deck. Matt took the lead, slowly raising his head above deck to take a cautious look around. At first, he could see and hear nothing, but a faint glimmer of light flashed across from the second boat wandering along the deck towards the wheelhouse. Matt relayed his observation to James in a hushed tone, and they slipped silently up the remaining steps, keeping below the gunnels.

Since they had gone to bed, the moon had disappeared and a thick band of cloud now covered the night sky. The darkness was intense and James felt a spatter of rain against his cheek as it began to drizzle.

"Can you see anything?" whispered James, his mouth close to Matt's ear.

"Not yet, but there's definitely someone here; somebody just entered the wheelhouse with their hand covering the torch," Matt whispered back.

"Let's wait here for the moment and watch," suggested James sensibly. "I'd bet money he's not alone."

The boys hunkered down, shifting their bodies so that they lay concealed by the gunnels, straining their ears above the rapid pounding of their hearts. A few minutes passed before a whispered voice followed by muffled footsteps, disturbed the silence. Five shadowy human forms moved aboard the second boat, berthed alongside. Less than six feet away from where Matt and James concealed position.

The voices continued to whisper animatedly until one of the shapes stretched out his leg and boarded the Matthew James, moored tightly alongside. The trespasser failed to see them as he crept along the deck towards the wheelhouse, but as a second visitor joined the first, the dim light from his torch picked out the boys as they huddled against the low wooden wall.

"Well, what a surprise," he almost whispered, the American drawl evident in his voice, more threatening than its soft tones. "Get up slowly; don't consider trying anything clever." He pointed a large menacing-looking revolver towards them.

Raising their hands, Matt and James rose slowly from their prone position, a mixture of fear and anger building inside them. They followed their captor's unspoken request as he gestured towards the wheelhouse with the weapon.

"Guess what I discovered hiding on the deck," he whispered, a gloating pleasure in his voice.

Panic threatened as dazzling torchlight caused momentary

blindness, destroying all sense of night vision. James could hear Matt struggling to keep his breathing slow and steady.

"These two are the boat's owners," whispered the first man hoarsely.

"Take them below and tie them up. Be careful, they're quite resourceful," he warned, as if he knew them.

They were shortly joined by the other men, who had boarded during the exchange. Shoved roughly through the hatch and down below deck, both James and Matt had their hands and feet tightly secured with rope found on their own deck. They were then bodily lifted and tossed onto the narrow bunks. With muttered exchanges, the assailants finished by swiftly sealing the boys' mouths with strong adhesive tape before returning to the deck, locking the hatch cover with a clank of bolts.

Matt had sighed arrogantly just before they sealed his mouth, and James gave a wry smile at his friend's bravery. Despite being trapped and trussed like Christmas turkeys, and without a clear means of escape, the relief they experienced at the withdrawal of the gun was huge.

Chapter 17:
The Colonel in Action

Maggie, speaking to the Colonel, informed him of everything that had happened. Like Matt and James, he was convinced something else was occurring behind the scenes.

Few realised the Colonel, during his military service, had served in the Intelligence Corps and was, in fact, a master strategist. His keen mind did not indicate his advancing years and, wishing to allay their concerns, he immediately started to formulate a plan of action. With the confidence befitting a man of his position, he told Maggie to stay at home, keep her ear to the ground and update him on any further developments.

After placing the telephone receiver back on its cradle, he sat back in the upright leather chair at his hardwood desk and stared into the dying flames of hi open fires for a few minutes. Then, picking up his fountain pen, he wrote a list in his neat italic handwriting. He knew that whatever he asked of his associates in the society, they would implement immediately.

Lifting the receiver again, Colonel Murray made his first call. His message to the Buchannan brothers in the next village was simple; to keep a vigil on the two boats at their mooring point on the loch, knowing that an attempt to catch Nessie would involve their use.

After making a string of calls to various people that lived around the loch closest to the Nessie sightings, he encouraged two of his most trusted associates to camp out above the area where Nessie's lair was suspected to be, knowing that this area was steep and, therefore, dangerous if you didn't know it well. They were told to be as discreet as possible and keep all signs of their presence hidden from casual observation.

Others were also told to camp in strategic places, close to roads, around the loch to monitor unusual activity and report back by radio.

The minute he had finished the calls, despite being very late in the evening, he went upstairs to change clothes. Opting for a set of combat fatigues, he hadn't worn in years; the Colonel was secretly pleasedwhen discovering they still fitted him well. With a quick, sideways glance in the mirror, he went outside, heading into the village towards the boarding house.

He knocked the back door gently and Maggie ushered him into the kitchen, shutting the door quietly.

"Guid evening, Colonel Murray. I'm very pleased to see ye."

"Guid evening, Maggie. I just wanted tae tell ye that I've set up watchin' stations all aroun' the loch at every conceivable point where somethin' might happen. Each manned by two of oor men, who'll observe the goin's on aroun' the loch until Ryan leaves fur good. If anythin' happens, we'll be the first tae know aboot it.

I'm just about tae do the rounds o' the most local stations tae ensure they have everythin' they need an' that they're camped in the most discreet spots. I'm already confident, but a guid leader always keeps in touch, reassuring his men he's with them, even when absence."

Maggie nodded before speaking. "It's been a good few year

since I've seen ye wearing yer uniform, Colonel. It brings back memories of when ye used tae visit me, when ye had leave."

The Colonel smiled. "Those days have long since gone, Maggie, but I remember them just as well. Twas a lifetime ago I served, and yet everythin' remains as fresh as yesterday, the accumulation of intelligence, the strategising, implementing the plan. I lived that way fur so long it's like I hav'nae been away from it."

"Just remember, ye're no as young these days, an' anything physical requires more effort. Ye be careful oot there, d'ye hear me?" warned Maggie, the demand is more than ye're used tae. The concern for her ageing friend genuine.

"Dinnae worry aboot me now, Maggie. I'm aware of ma physical limitations, but it's always good tae hear yer concern for ma well-bein', an' that's somethin' else that has'nae altered with the passin' o' the years."

He bade her goodnight and slipped out the way he had come.

"I've always liked the way ye looked in uniform, Colonel!" she said softly to his departing back. If he heard, he may have turned and seen her expression, part-wistful, part-concerned, but Colonel Murray continued along the path that led to the Matthew James, until he noticed a man walking towards him. Drawing closer, he recognised the figure as Neil Buchannan and raised his hand in recognition.

Neil wasted no time in greeting. "I'm glad ye're here, Colonel. Matt and James have had visitors, none too pleasant."

"What's happened, Neil? Start at the beginning an' spare no details, I need tae know everythin'," the Colonel said firmly.

"We set up camp 20 yards o' the boat in less than an hour from yer phone call. We decided that we could afford tae be so close because there is little reason for anyone tae come along the path beyond the boats. We found a secure spot amongst the trees that gave us excellent concealment but still enabled us tae see the boats perfectly well.

"We took turns tae watch from a forward observation point an', at about half past nine, five very rough-looking men appeared an' went on board the boats. They seemed tae be checking things oot an' were very thorough in their work. Anyway, after aboot half an hour they left, goin' back towards the village an' then the boys returned to their boat. They went below deck, asleep by now I should think. The men hav'nae returned, an' I came tae let ye know. Andrew is watchin' them as we speak."

"Somethin' is going doon tonight and tha's fur sure. I'd hazard a guess they knew Matt and Jimmy were no aboard, then probably warned by radio that they were returning from the boardin' house, probably why they left. Ma guess is they intended tae take the boat, but with Matt an' Jimmy aboot to return, the alarm was sounded an' led to them dispersing. Nae, I think that they'll return when the lads are asleep, so our friends are in danger."

"Do you think their lives are at risk?" Neil asked. "Maybe, but probably not," reasoned the Colonel.

"If this were ma operation, then I would want tae take them alive. First, it would prolong the time they had wi' the boat afore it was discovered missin', and second, hostages could be useful if somethin' goes wrong. But, if whatever they're plannin' is completed afore the morning, it would shed a different light on their situation. If so, their need for them is reduced and yer guess is as guid as mine what they'll do next."

"Fur now, let's get tae yer observation point, an' check in wi' yer brother."

Neil led the way, turning away from the moored boats as they approached, to prevent their silhouettes appearing against the background of the loch. They went straight to the observation point where Andrew crouched in silent concentration.

As the Colonel was convinced something would happen

117

shortly, he decided to wait with the brothers. The moonlit night sky continued to cloud over, making it increasingly difficult to see, and so they decided to have two of them on lookout duty, while the third rested.

Shortly after two o'clock in the morning, during the brief time when all three observers were together changing shifts, they spotted a group of men walking silently along the wooden jetty. At a gesture from Andrew, they crouched down to ensure they were completely hidden.

The five paid no attention to the Matthew James as they boarded the larger boat and disappeared into the wheelhouse. Only one man returned, who proceeded to carefully go through the supplies on deck, for nearly half an hour, without making a sound, his presence only indicated by an occasional shaft of torch light.

The man on deck eventually crossed onto the Matthew James and started to examine the remaining supplies, yet to be transferred to the larger boat. Just as he was stepping back between the two, he dropped his torch, which clunked onto the deck in darkness, rolling a few feet back towards the wheelhouse. The watchers heard and witnessed the man stoop and grope around for it. Spotting it in the dark, he stretched out his hand to grab it but misjudged the distance and instead sent it rolling further across the deck. When he finally picked it up, he returned to the others in the wheelhouse.

Then the watchers noticed Matt and James emerging from the hatch to crawl beneath the gunnels of their boat, the boys obviously aware that something was wrong. With clenched teeth, they witnessed Matt and James being threatened with the gun and taken below deck. They saw the captors seal the hatch cover, step back aboard the Katie Marie and heard the starting motor turn over as the engine fired into life. The vessel moved off slowly with a low rumbling, its darkness giving the boat a ghost-like quality as it moved across the loch.

After waiting two minutes for the fading sound to change pitch, the boat sped up. The concealed observers had watched and listened enough. They knew that the coast was clear and stood up, stretching their limbs from their cramped positions.

"It's time tae release oor friends and see if they're alright," the Colonel announced, moving towards the jetty.

Aboard the boat, he pulled back the bolts securing the hatch cover, lifted it, and made his way down the steep stairs. His hand knocked against a switch, which immediately illuminated the space below deck with a soft glow. Spotting James and Matt bound and gagged on their bunks, he quickly stripped off the tape covering their mouths.

"That's what I call good timing, Colonel," said Matt warmly, smiling at the older man.

"We saw it all fae where we were watchin', so it was just a case o' waitin' for them tae leave afore we could release ye. Are either of ye hurt?"

"We're fine. They were rough getting us down here; we'll probably have a few bruises, but that's all," James assured him.

The Colonel briefed them, receiving a thumbs-up from Matt at his carefully laid plans. Having left in such haste earlier, the next task was to finish distributing walkie-talkies to the rest of the observers. It was crucial that he could remain in contact with them all, over the coming hours. As the Buchannan brothers were no longer needed here, he sent them back to his house to collect the radio handsets, reminding them to keep out of sight as much as possible.

Matt and James, of course, had their boat's inbuilt radio to rely on, and it was this that the Colonel would utilise to run the operation. He had the bit firmly between his teeth now and was already planning his next move.

119

Chapter 18:
To Catch a Plesiosaur

Once the Colonel had released the captives and organised the Buchannan brothers, the boat thieves were over half-way across the loch, preparing for the next phase of their operation.

Aboard, two men sat on the gunnels in full diving apparatus, watching two more spread out the massive net. The fifth, clearly the leader of the group, stood in the wheelhouse, steering and barking out orders. Approaching the cliff face, he shut down the engines, skillfully allowing the boat to glide gracefully to a stop twenty yards short of the cliff.

The divers stood up clumsily and let themselves topple backwards into the water where they waited for the net to be fed to them. Taking an end each, they disappeared into the murky depths of the loch, the phosphorescent glow emitted by their underwater lights gradually fading as they disappeared further from the undulating surface of the water.

Swimming down, the divers swung their torches sideways, searching for the ledge of the overhang that Marty had predicted. At a signal from the lead diver indicating he had spotted something, both men swam towards the shoreline, approaching a dark, cavernous space below the rocky wall. With excited nods and gesticulations but the laziest of kicks with their flippers, they made their way along the opening to find out its length, before noisily hammering the net into position using metal pegs stored in the utility belts at their waists, until the heavy meshwork hung down, covering the recess below.

It was only when they moved back to survey their completed handiwork, that they finally realised the enormity of their undertaking; somewhere behind the net lay Nessie, the plesiosaur, who was undoubtedly aware of this pair of trespassers invading her territory!

Tugging their safety lines alerted those above that they were ready to return to the safety of the boat They both breathed a sigh of relief as their heads broke the surface, and heard the excited chatter of the crew. Nodding in acknowledgement of the adrenaline rush of danger they had just experienced, they made an unspoken agreement; no one would hear of the gut-wrenching fear they'd felt at this monstrous reptile's presence as they engaged in their subaquatic task.

At the boarding house, Marty was woken suddenly by a noise from the adjacent room; Ryan's. Instantly alert, he dressed hurriedly and was already lacing his boots when he heard the familiar squeak of the other man's door. This was followed by the stairs creaking as Ryan descended to ground level. At the soft clunk of the front door closing, Marty crossed the landing to Pete's room to rouse him.

Instructing his friend to get dressed, he then warned the others, Marty suggested they met outside and followed Ryan together. His instinct warned the man might be dangerous, he was executing his plans and was anxious to capture Nessie. Quickly alerting Lucy, he told her to wake Maggie before racing downstairs to hunt out a torch. Pete joined him outside shortly afterwards, tugging a sweater over his head as he pulled the door to.

Hearing Ryan's painstaking progress along the gravel driveway, Marty guessed he was going for the truck; his suspicions were confirmed when he heard a door open and clunk softly closed, as Ryan climbed into the cab.

"We'll lose him straight away if we don't get onto that truck," urged Pete.

"Let's just hang on to the tailboard," suggested Marty. "If we crouch down low, he won't be able to see us."

Keeping low and opposite the driver's side, they crept towards the rear of the truck, reaching it as the engine spluttered into life. In the pulse of adrenaline, they did not question the wisdom of their decision, climbing onto the tow bar and gripping tightly to the tail gate as the truck lurched forward, sending gravel spraying upwards behind it.

Lucy, watching from a distance, ran back inside to tell Maggie who immediately picked up her walkie-talkie to reach Colonel Murray. He called to Matt and James, waiting patiently below deck, although this time, with the hatch open! They heard that Ryan had left the boarding house and was probably heading towards them.

"It's ma guess, boys, that oor friends on the other boat are goin' tae try an' catch Nessie tonight, an' that Ryan is on his way tae meet 'em. He must be feelin' pretty certain of her capture 'cause there's only a couple of hours o' the night left. How he's goin' tae achieve it, I dinnae ken, but he's goin' tae need a mighty large vehicle tae move a creature o' that size back on land, an' plenty o' manpower tae help get her oot o' the watter. So, we have tae think smart, an' wait for the right opportunity afore we try tae stop him.

"We cannae let him get Nessie oot o' the watter, fur I cannae imagine that he's intendin' tae keep her alive. If we knew his tactics for catching her, we could run interference."

Matt looked thoughtful. "Well, he knows roughly where Nessie disappears to and he'd probably use the net we had on the boat to snare her. If he covered the entrance to Nessie's lair, she'll accidentally swim into it when she leaves. The problem is, they can't anticipate when she'll do that."

"Then I suppose they'll have to force her out. But how?" asked James, bewildered.

"We dinnae have time at oor liberty tae talk this through right now," said the Colonel, putting an end to further discussion.

"We need tae get into position to intervene quickly if required. Matt, I want ye tae set a course across the loch, north of their position, as best as ye can guess, an' oot o' their hearing. Then I want ye tae put the boat on a collision course with them an' cut the engines, bringing us as close as ye can withoot letting them know that we're there. Can ye do that?"

"You place a twenty pence piece on a mark and I'll park the boat right on top of it for you, Colonel, and that's a guarantee!" Matt told him confidently.

"A twenty wha'?"

"Oh, nothing…" Matt cursed himself for not remembering that decimal money hadn't been brought in yet!

Maggie heard from the Colonel, asking her to radio the look-outs and inform them of current events. She contacted many watching from the opposite side of the loch and moved them to reinforce other teams. She also told them to be on the lookout for a large vehicle capable of transporting a creature about thirty feet long and weighing several tons. The vehicle might carry a team of Ryan's men, likely to be armed and dangerous. She instructed them not to approach, for any reason.

After the calls ended, Lucy said she wanted to find Pete. Maggie was initially reluctant, but she knew that the two photographers had become firm friends over their shared interest, despite the difference in their ages. Maggie didn't want to miss any action either; she acquiesced and suggested they went together,

123

following the route Ryan had taken. Although she hadn't needed to drive her ageing Morris car for some time, she decided to get it out of the garage to avoid further delay.

On board the boat, the divers removed their wetsuits, and waited for new instructions along with those who pulled them from the depths a short while ago. The wheelhouse radio crackled as a message from Ryan arrived, hastily answered by the leader of the group who had joined them on deck.

"Ryan says to wait for him before waking Nessie, so everything's got to be ready when he gives the go-ahead. Check the net-towing ropes are secure, and the devices are ready and primed."

The men nodded, checking the ropes, while others opened a crate and pulled out several tubular canisters, the size of a five-gallon oil drum.

The leader watched them work, slowly smoking the remains of a cigar and expelling the acrid smoke skywards. Confident that everything was progressing smoothly, he returned to the radio in the wheelhouse to check that the six men, waiting half a mile away on the flatbed lorry, were also ready.

Shortly after this, Ryan's truck approached the group of men and their vehicle. As it slowed down, Marty risked peering round the side of the truck from his position on the tailgate. He leaned towards Pete and called loudly in his ear that they would have to jump for it, if they wanted to avoid being seen. The truck slowed as Ryan applied the brakes and the two men jumped, breaking their falls by rolling, like parachutists, towards the track. Uninjured, they reached the cover of the bushes without being spotted, quickly following the truck to observe the men's activities.

The lorry had reversed to the water's edge and ramps stretched outwards into the water. A long, thick winch cable extended the full length of the flatbed vehicle and lay with the huge hooked end at the water's edge.

The six men were sitting on the edge of the flatbed in a row, waiting patiently for their next task. Ryan parked the truck at the edge of the track, almost totally in bushes, allowing room for the lorry to pass, before leaving it and greeting the men.

He spoke impatient instructions, actioning his plans as less than two hours of darkness remained. Taking the radio from one of them, he summoned the men on the boat.

"Set the charges off," he ordered quietly. His eyes were aglow, knowing that this simple instruction would begin the sequence of events leading to the capture of Nessie and, thus, his own fame and fortune.

The leader in the wheelhouse came onto the deck and ordering a pair of canisters deployed. Everyone watched as the first one was loaded into a small catapult device and sent hurtling towards the cliff. The canister entered the depths with a small splash considering its large size and disappeared from view. The catapult operator counted off the seconds before the muffled roar rumbled, and the loch surface erupted into a plume of water thirty feet high, before cascading loudly back into the loch. A moment of silence was followed by the second canister exploding, before silence reigned.

The men watched the net ropes carefully, waiting for them to tighten, signifying that the monster had been caught, but they remained hanging limply off the side of the boat.

Two more charges were expelled by the catapult, and further plumes of water erupted from the loch close to the cliff edge. However, a vicious pull on the net ropes lurched the boat violently sideways. The quarry was in the net! A moment of stunned silence passed before a loud cheer erupted. Ryan sat down woodenly, his eyes staring, as the men thumped him excitedly on the back. Nobody noticed his tears threatening to overspill.

Glancing briefly down at him from his position at the

wheel, the leader impassively turned the ignition on the engine, and the boat moved quietly away.

Two hundred yards away, the Matthew James waited silently. The occupants had heard everything and now realised the truth, that they were using explosives to frighten Nessie from her lair. The minute they heard the boat's engine, Matt started theirs, knowing its sound was masked by the noise of the other. He set off in pursuit. The Colonel's face was grim, and he struggled to hide the anger burning deep inside him. He felt helpless, knowing without doubt, that Ryan had captured Nessie. He hoped more than anything that he could save the creature, before Ryan murdered her.

Chapter 19:
Who is the Loch Ness Monster?

Maggie and the girls followed the same route that Ryan had taken, but the ancient car found the going hard, especially after leaving the main road and joining the rough track leading to the loch. The car was misbehaving, regularly misfiring, the sound of which travelled distance on such calm nights. Maggie decided to abandon it about half a mile from where she believed Ryan would be waiting.

They took to foot, which was also difficult with Lorna's injury to consider. She didn't complain though; after her recent confinement, she welcomed being outside and involved again. She used her twin's shoulder for support on one side, and an old wooden walking stick on the other and kept her bad foot off the ground.

Maggie set the pace and led slightly ahead of the girls, her fiercely protective nature towards them evident. Besides, she still retained excellent hearing and could alert them if anything was amiss.

Little light illuminated the way, but knowing the route from past visits to the inlet helped, and they covered the ground quickly.

When the flatbed lorry came into sight, Maggie stopped where Marty and Pete had jumped from Ryan's truck. She waited for the girls to catch up and suggested that they hide in the bushes so they could watch what happened. Without realizing it, they were five yards from where Pete and Marty hid. Neither emerged to greet them, aware of something the women weren't.

Crouching amongst the foliage, the silence was broken abruptly by a voice from behind, ordering them to stand and move forward. Initially, they remained frozen to the spot, but when the instruction was repeated, Maggie accepted the inevitable, they were caught. She stood, leaving the cover of the bushes, and faced an ugly brute of a man aiming a handgun directly towards her. The twins quickly followed, Lorna gasped as she noticed the gun.

"Down there!" said the brute, pointing towards the lorry with the gun.

Not wanting to antagonise the gunman, Maggie led the twins down the track. She was barely surprised when a figure, turning round to face them, revealed himself to be John Ryan.

"Maggie and the lovely twins! This is indeed a surprise! How nice of you to come and witness my great achievement. Nessie will arrive shortly and taken by lorry to a secret location for examination. You realise it's a plesiosaur and probably the world's sole living dinosaur. Not only accredited with the capture of a live dinosaur but also with solving one of Scotland's greatest mysteries. I'll receive the recognition I've long deserved, being the modern world's greatest explorer and investigator of strange phenomena."

"Ye're countin' yer chickens afore they hatch, Mr Ryan, because Nessie is'nae gonna give up withoot a fight, tha's fur sure," Maggie told him angrily.

"You're incorrect, madam, it's contained in my net and travels here, now."

"How do you propose to keep her alive, Ryan?" asked

Lucy. "I don't see any water tank on your lorry."

"Alas, the misfortune of catching such a vast creature means that I have no tank large enough to put it in," answered Ryan, a simulated expression of sadness on his face. "Dead or alive, the creature will grant my desires, so it's superfluous!"

"You are completely despicable, Ryan. What gives you the right to decide whether this creature lives or dies?" cried Lorna angrily. "Especially one of this significance!"

"The right is mine, honey, because I finance operations, and make the decisions," Ryan told her. "Now, please excuse me, there are matters requiring my attention."

Turning his back on the group, he made his way down to the water's edge. "Tie them up and gag them," he shouted as he disappeared from view.

Marty and Pete had witnessed the proceedings, and they weren't the only ones.

Nessie was thrashing about in the net, unaware of the injury she could cause herself. With her flippers pinned against her great body, she used her massively powerful tail to beat the surrounding water, attempting to free herself from this encumbrance.

The boat rocked violently, making it almost impossible to steer in the direction the pilot wanted. He fought it constantly, but the journey, just a few minutes' duration, took longer than anyone expected. Since the creature was still completely submerged, he could not anticipate the moves she made, in order to compensate for them quickly enough, and was forced to slew the wheel repeatedly in his attempt to prevent a capsize. He radioed through to the shore to express his difficulties, but Ryan simply ordered him to get there as quickly as he could. He replaced the radio handset despondently, knowing that the morning light would break before the creature was loaded onto the lorry.

Finally, light from a torch flashing some way ahead of the

boat indicated how far he had to go before he reached his destination, and he sighed in relief as he calculated it to be about 200 yards. He considered dropping another depth charge to stun the creature again, but decided against it in case he damaged the net. There was nothing he could do except doggedly continue his route.

Back on shore, Ryan found it difficult to contain his excitement as he saw the torchlight from the boat responding to his own communication; he was so close now to accomplishing his dream. Taking a deep breath, attempting to still his rapidly beating heart, he instructed one of his men to let out more line from the lorry's winch, in readiness for the next part of the operation. His eyes didn't leave the boat, which had just appeared from the darkness, observing the crazy course it was taking. He understood the difficulty of positioning the boat to ease the net transfer to the winch. The tension required removing from the tethers first, meaning Nessie needed beaching in the correct place. His whole operation rested with his old and trusted friend, battling the creature's boat side.

On board the Matthew James, the Colonel had deployed all his available support people around the area, people Ryan had mistakenly believed he could command. Like a grandmaster of chess, he continually repositioned his men, placing each one closer and closer to their target, in anticipation of the final confrontation that, in his opinion, was inevitable. Matt and James marveled at the calm way he considered everything thoroughly before taking action, and commented that he held promise to become a great rugby coach.

He had foreseen the positioning of Ryan's boat would be critical for Nessie's removal from the water, and hoped the Matthew James could make achieving that position more difficult.

He had decided that the last course of action would be to ram the stolen boat and beach it, making it impossible for Ryan to retrieve his catch.

The night's darkness would soon pass and their presence beside the larger boat would be discovered before the opportunity to attempt the tactics he wanted to implement. It was the element of surprise that he wanted to keep beyond anything else.

The boat towing Nessie had finally reached the beach where Ryan was waiting. As the shore sloped upwards, the creature appeared, and the sheer size of it terrified the men aboard. The massive tail still beat the water in defiance, but now the creature raised it high before crashing it down onto the surface with such force that it sent water almost as high as the depth charges had done earlier.

The man at the wheel shifted the gears between forward and reverse, edging the boat and the plesiosaur ever closer to the beach, until he felt the boat cease its sideways slide and he knew that he had done it, Nessie was beached. Nessie appeared to give up fighting, her tail stopped beating, and she lay motionless, the hump of her body proud of the water.

The net ropes slackened and Ryan ordered two men to wade out with the winch hook. The chosen men appeared hesitant at getting into the water, close to the huge beast, but followed their orders without question and passed over the hook.

Prior to the ropes being transferred, a roar from the engine of the Matthew James announced their presence. They had crept closer without drawing the attention of Ryan's men. One man stood by the wheel, two waited on deck to board the larger boat.

The look on the Colonel's face was one of total commitment as he rammed the larger boat in the stern, causing it to twist violently and the slack in the nets' tethers to tighten in response.

At the precise moment of contact, Matt and James jumped

aboard, avoiding the violence of the collision while in the air. Charging at two of Ryan's men, they sent them flying overboard with such force that they only just prevented themselves from following. The victims struck the water with the air sucked from their chests, struggling to stay afloat as they gasped for the oxygen their lungs just couldn't seem to take in.

James launched himself at another man, sending him on the same water-bound journey as his previous target, but Matt wasn't so lucky. His target twisted instinctively, grabbing the hem of Matt's sweater, swinging him around and off-balance. A fist connected with his shoulder, deadening the muscle instantly, but it scarcely made any difference. Injuries were commonplace when playing rugby, and Matt had experienced many. He ducked underneath the next blow and brought his head up sharply, connecting hard with his assailant's chin. The man was unconscious before he slumped to the deck.

James was already on his way to the wheelhouse before Matt could follow, but suddenly stopped short and retreated as an extended arm with a gun appeared from the wheelhouse, followed by the complete form of an old friend who moved slowly out onto the deck.

"Hello boys! Surprised to see me? I should have known that you'd turn up. To be honest, I'm sick to death at the sight of you," said a familiar icy-cold voice.

"How did *you* get back here, Heart?" Matt asked him, equally coldly.

"I never really left. Those dumb cops just thought I did."

Another voice from behind them spoke. "I'm here to capture the Loch Ness Monster and I will complete my mission. Focus your attention on the beach, boys, see what else I caught earlier," Ryan grinned as he boarded.

Matt and James glanced ashore to see Maggie, and the twins shackled and gagged, each had a gun pointed at their heads.

James felt the rage build inside him.

"You think that's the Loch Ness Monster?" he asked menacingly, pointing at Nessie.

"Of course, boy! What kind of question is that?" drawled Ryan haughtily.

"You're wrong! It's a harmless creature that's survived in the loch for millennia, never bothering anyone, or hurting them. Let me identify the real Loch Ness Monster. It's simple really, you're the Loch Ness Monster, Ryan! You and others like you who are only interested in themselves and possible gains. You don't give a damn about anyone else!" he finished.

Ryan looked at him and laughed maniacally. It was the insane laughter of a madman, sending shivers down the spines of everyone there.

Chapter 20:
The Power of the People

The Colonel witnessed everything from the wheelhouse and realised it was time to escalate proceedings. He strode across the deck and stepped over to the other boat.

"What's the meanin' of this ootrage?" he said, walking up to Heart. "Put that gun away before somebody gets hurt!"

"Stay where you are, you meddling old fool, or you'll be the first to get it," Heart snarled at him.

Matt and James edged around so that they stood next to the Colonel. The Colonel held a small walkie-talkie in his hand and discreetly pressed the 'transmit' button three times. Matt distinctly heard the radio in the wheelhouse click three times as it received the signal. He knew what it signified. Heart was standing between them and the shore with his back towards it.

"I said stay where you are, or I won't hesitate to pull the trigger," Heart barked for a second time.

"You will not pull that trigger, Heart, because you're outnumbered. Look behind you?" Matt said, far too confidently for Heart's liking.

"I might have fallen for that trick once, but I won't be

falling for it again," he replied, the sneer on his face extending right up to his ears.

"Oh, it's no trick, Heart. Humour me please, look behind you," James joined in.

"Yer position here is temporary, Heart. How many bullets in your gun? Six? It's no goin' tae be enough fur everyone behind ye," the Colonel said, politely. "Now, be a good chap and give me the gun."

"Shut up, you old fool! *I* have the gun so *I'll* give the orders," Heart shouted, starting to lose his temper.

"Oh dear, Matt! It appears Mr Heart's temper is as bad as Mr Ryan's. They really are two of a kind, aren't they?" James tormented Heart further.

Heart raised his arm to strike James, when a thunderous shot rang out and buckshot flew above his head. Heart reacted immediately, whirling around to locate the source of the shot, so Matt and James took advantage of his break in concentration by charging at his back. The force of their dual attack sent his gun flying into the air, swiftly followed by Heart himself, plunging into the cold waters of the loch right next to the hapless netted creature. The animal lifted its tail, whipping it swiftly up and down, catching the side of Heart's bobbing head, immediately rendering him unconscious. He was quickly dragged from the water by two thugs standing on the beach.

"Two for two where Heart is concerned, James," Matt grinned.

Ryan had been watching the confrontation between the boys and Heart with mounting enjoyment. High time they received their comeuppance and continued to watch what Heart did next. He hadn't quite expected the turn of events however, and shuffled away, gaining distance between them. As he moved, the Colonel commanded him to stand still.

"I don't take orders from people like you, Colonel

Murray."

"I came to that conclusion a while ago, Ryan, but like yer pal, Heart, I am goin' tae invite ye also tae take a wee peek behind ye, it'll be in yer best interests, I assure ye."

For a moment, Ryan looked hesitant but turned his head despite himself. He saw the unconscious Heart lying at the water's edge, and the three men covering the women with their weapons. The other four watched on with interest.

"What exactly is it you want me to look at?" asked Ryan sarcastically.

"Watch!" the Colonel said simply, and he walked to the edge of the boat and stood above Nessie.

Silently, people started to emerge from the bushes in pairs, making their way to the water. At first ten appeared, then twenty. They were followed by a huge number until every member of the Loch Ness Preservation Society stood behind the captive women. Ryan couldn't believe what he saw. His shoulders slumped as he realised the futility of his situation.

Colonel Murray addressed the six men on the beach. "Gentlemen, I would like ye tae put doon yer weapons an' release yer captives because frankly, I would'nae like tae see the effect should one of ye happen tae let off a shot or harm the ladies."

The crowd behind the thugs began talking, and the thugs turned instantly to see who made the noise. A few seconds passed before they realised they held no chance against such numbers. They placed their weapons on the ground and were quickly surrounded by the throng.

The Colonel and the boys failed to witness what happened after, but Matt supposed they were not handled too gently.

The Colonel turned to a silent and defeated Ryan. "It's over Mr Ryan; ye're no welcome here anymore. We will escort ye an' yer people tae the nearest police station where I imagine ye'll be held for questionin'. If ye're lucky enough tae walk away fae all this a free man, then yer equipment and vehicle will be awaitin' ye. As Chairman of our society, I will tell ye now that ye'll ne'er set foot here again, an' if you try, well, let's just say that accidents happen, if ye ken what I mean. Ye've no exactly made many friends here now, have ye?"

He forced Ryan ashore with Matt and James as escorts, and handed him over to the awaiting horde to take care of on their way to the station. Then he called the Buchannan brothers over to assist with the next job.

James climbed down from the boat, while Matt clambered ashore more clumsily, his shoulder starting to feel painful and stiff from the blow it had received. They both embraced the three women, just being untied by Marty and Pete. Satisfied they were unharmed, James returned to the Colonel.

"We need to release poor Nessie, Colonel. We can't let her remain out of the water for much longer, she's suffered enough already."

"Already on'tae it, ma boy. I've asked the Buchannan boys tae join us on board for extra manpower. What we'll do is tow poor Nessie out tae deeper water and cut the ropes connected tae the net. With any luck, the poor thing'll be able tae shake it off and swim away back tae where she belongs."

"Sounds like a sensible plan, Colonel," replied James, and went to reverse the smaller boat from blocking their access to the loch.

Matt started the more powerful engine on the larger vessel, then began pulling Nessie from the beach. At first the huge creature didn't appear to be moving but, as he increased the throttle, the extra power gradually inched Nessie down the shore and into deeper water.

The great creature did not struggle, and the Colonel feared for her health. She was exhausted, she probably couldn't free herself from the net.

When they had travelled a sufficient distance from the shore, the Colonel gave the order to stop the engines. The Buchannan brothers tethered the Matthew James alongside the larger boat and stepped aboard.

"Cut the ropes!" ordered the Colonel.

Neil produced a knife, setting to work on the thick material. It was painstakingly slow work, especially as the net was pulled so tight by the creature's immense weight.

Finally, the first rope broke free, the last few strands snapping under the force of its load.

James observed the creature lying just under the water's surface. "She's not breaking free; I think the poor thing's exhausted," he said, worriedly.

Neil worked the other rope, doggedly sawing away, but James saw at least two of the creature's fin-like limbs remained tangled within the mesh of the net. He called out to Neil to stop and explained the problem.

"If we release the net now, I don't believe Nessie has enough strength to free her limbs. We'll have to free her by hand, which means getting into the water alongside her."

"That sounds pretty dangerous, James. Even if we were able tae untangle the poor creature, there's a chance that ye'd be caught up in the net an' dragged doon tae the bottom wi'it."

"It's a risk we must take, Colonel, and honestly, this definitely requires more man-power."

The Colonel considered James' comments before deciding, he nodded thoughtfully.

"I agree with yer assessment, laddie. We'll need three of us, with sharp knives, tae achieve that, and I'll nae order anyone tae risk their lives on a potentially lethal mission."

"Orders are not required, Colonel. Matt and I will volunteer, it's the only course of action available," James told him, determination etched on his face.

"We're goin' as well, Colonel. We took an oath tae protect the loch years ago, when ye invited us tae join the preservation society. The loch has provided us wi' a home an' a livin', an' noo we can show oor appreciation of it," stated Neil, purposefully.

"In that case I'm goin' tae come, too," said the Colonel.

"I'm afraid you cannae, Colonel. Someone has to stay an' manoeuvre the boat an' take care of the safety lines that we'll be attached tae. Tae be honest, I can think of no other I'd rather trust my life with," Neil told him gently.

The Colonel appreciated his comment; the trust that the four were placing in him helped ease his initial disappointment. He realised he was years beyond the peak of his physical prowess, and that the task was best suited to the young and fit.

The first light of dawn spread its pastel-pink tendrils across the sky, announcing the start of a particularly beautiful day. Matt glanced across to the shoreline and witnessed a swathe of loch inhabitants standing by, watching. Ryan and his cohorts had vanished, and Matt assumed they were arrested and escorted away.

Colonel Murray radioed his people, telling them what they were intending to do, and as Matt, James and the Buchannans stripped off their outer clothes, they heard a cheer from the shore. Looking back, they saw every one of them raise an arm to salute, their bravery. They understood the risk.

Matt and James looked at each other with raised eyebrows,

"If our teammates realised what we get involved with, I wonder what their response might be," muttered James, taking up a position on the gunnels.

With safety lines secured around their waists, the four dived into the water. They worked in pairs, each working on one of the limbs towards the top of the net. Within minutes they had cut away enough net to free them, but the remaining two presented a serious problem. Situated under the creature's bulk, meant the

139

rescuers had to work underwater, with the added risk that Nessie might drag them under if she could suddenly free herself and swim off.

So far, the creature had barely moved; she just lay in the water, despite having the four of them around her. Matt wondered if she knew they were trying to help her or if she was just too exhausted to care. He swam underneath the creature to check how badly snared she was and returned with positive news that she was held by a single limb.

Light was penetrating the water's depths but insufficient to work with, so Matt called to the Colonel for an underwater torch which was duly supplied. Then, still in pairs, they took turns, one holding the light whilst their partner sawed at the net, until their task was complete.

Still, Nessie lay atop the net, but the need to stay in the cold water had passed. The four returned to the boat and climbed aboard with the Colonel's help, shivering violently. They were greeted again by great cheers from the crowd.

"If we tie the net to the boat and move away slowly, we would unroll Nessie and prevent the net falling to the bottom of the loch," James suggested.

The Colonel liked the idea but stated his concerns for Nessie, still worried about the creature's apparent weakened state.

"What if we tow her aroun' fur a bit an' try tae re-oxygenate her?" Neil suggested.

"Like we do when we release a fish that we've caught, you mean?" James asked.

"It's worth a try, it *has* tae be," Neil replied.

Strong ropes were secured around the plesiosaur, and Matt asked Colonel Murray to steer the boat, in case they were required back in the water. The Colonel took the helm proudly and steered a circular course for twenty minutes while everyone watched the creature for signs of improvement.

"It's working, boys, Nessie is startin' tae move aboot," shouted Neil suddenly, with a mixture of relief and delight. He was right; they saw her flippers stretching back and forth, as if regaining feeling.

James asked the Colonel to stop the boat. "It's time to release her, Colonel."

The Colonel left the wheelhouse, joining them as they cut the tow lines. Nessie, sensing her freedom, rolled to her side and entered the depths of the loch, leaving the tangled net hanging from the side of the boat.

She was free again!

Chapter 21:
Retribution

Despite having been up all night, the Colonel continued to drive forward a series of plans that had no obvious meaning to anybody else. Such was the level of respect he commanded, that few ever argued with him or questioned his schemes. Matt and James listened to a whole string of calls he made journeying back to their moorings. They were totally bemused by what he instigated.

As they docked, he instructed everyone to sleep, then meet him on the far side of the loch. Before returning to the boarding house, he shook hands with the boys, thanking them for everything they had done and telling them that it was definitely time that they, and the twins, joined his society.

The boys went down below and crawled into their bunks, asleep in seconds beneath the blankets.

Several hours later, the twins were sent to rouse them and, together, they travelled across the loch. A buzz of activity permeated the area already, and several people were setting up an assortment of equipment onto a large truck, similar to the one Ryan had used, alongside a full-sized model of Nessie.

Matt looked at James, saying, "You can't tell me that they made that this morning while we were asleep!"

James scratched his forehead, "Well, Nessie's obviously been appearing around here for a while, for anyone to have constructed such an accurate replica. No chance this was a lucky guess!"

The Colonel came over to greet them.

"Good morning, Colonel Murray!" said James. "What's going on?"

"G'mornin', lads! Well, it's a simple matter o'retribution, ma boy. We're going tae film Nessie in the net an' slip a copy into Ryan's bag afore he leaves Scotland. He'll think he's won the jackpot when he discovers it an' will be sure tae release it, only tae have it proved a fake! That will discredit or, at least, place a certain amount of doubt on his 'evidence'.

"At the moment, he's still being held in Inverness, thanks tae oor friends in the force, but there's a limit tae the length of time he can be held without charges, so we need tae act quickly tae get this done. The punishment is to expose Ryan as a fraud; more difficult fur him tae bear than a spell in prison."

The Colonel looked so pleased with himself that both boys found themselves grinning.

"You certainly know how to get things done, Colonel!"
"Everyone who took the oath tae protect what we have here, is totally committed tae our cause. They're an amazing group of people tae represent an' lead. Have ye thought about joining us yerselves, yet? I know we only discussed it briefly, but the society could do wi' some fresh young blood."

"We haven't discussed it, Colonel, but I doubt there will be any problem there," James told him.

"What do you want us to do, Colonel?" asked Matt.

"Ye lads have done enough already. There's little fur ye tae do but sit back an' enjoy the show! Then with a little creative ingenuity fae oor new friend, Pete Jackson, we should have oor little gift for Mr Ryan by tonight and be able tae send him on his way."

The Nessie model was positioned carefully in the heavy net, still hanging from the Matthew James, and in the same beached position the real Nessie adopted, several hours ago.

Then, with some creative interpretation, Pete and Lucy filmed the scene from different angles before the creature was retrieved, loaded onto the lorry and driven off. Lucy and Pete drove off too with their rolls of film, back to the boarding house.

"Colonel, how will the film be proved a fake?" asked James, suddenly curious.

"It's very simple really; one edge of Nessie's tail bears a message fae the people of Loch Ness in very wee print. It will only be revealed under close scrutiny. It may well be tha' it's no discovered fur several weeks, but one thing fur certain is that sometime in the future, all o' Mr Ryan's claims will be discredited an' he will be derided within the academic community. Tae be honest, it could'nae happen tae a nicer chap, could it noo?"

"What's the wording, 'Made in China'?" asked Matt.

"A grand idea! But we thought we'd make it a wee bit more personal. It reads: 'To the *real* Loch Ness Monster, John Ryan, with fond memories from the people o' the Loch.' It was Maggie's idea; she wanted tae add a few X's, but I managed tae talk her oot of it! I think she's a grand woman, but thank goodness she listens tae sense!"

Matt and James both laughed at the image, at the moment of realization, on Ryan's face when the message was discovered.

"He'll never be taken seriously again; he'll be a complete laughing stock!" said Matt.

"Aye, he will, but he deserves everythin' tha's comin' tae him.

"Well, lads, yer new homes will be ready in a couple o'

144

weeks, an' I reckon at least two young lassies would like tae spend time there with ye," teased the Colonel.

Matt and James grinned at him and walked over towards Pete and Lucy.

Matt looked sideways at his friend. "I reckon Lucy is just at the beginning of a brand new photographic career, you know!"

James was looking thoughtful. "They'd probably make a good team together.

"Matt, I think we've done what we came here to do.

An hour later, the boys left the boat, and strolled along the trail towards the field that led to the woods. Strangely, the journey didn't seem as long as the first time and, once they passed through the forest, they soon reached the waterfall.

"It's been a great adventure!" said James as they clambered up the rocks, sitting down to absorb the beautiful view one final time.

"I feel like we made a real difference here and I liked being the characters we were. I, for one, am going to miss Maggie's cooking, the girl's smiles, the peace around the loch, and I really liked having our own boat," he continued. "It might sound strange, but I quite liked the Colonel too. I'd have enjoyed getting to know him better. He's a pretty cool customer if you ask me, and I bet he has a million cool stories from the war."

"What was your favourite part of the adventure Matt?"

"Perhaps a little bit weird but although I enjoyed the physical side of the adventure, meeting so many decent people and, for a while, being part of their team was cool."

"I know exactly what you mean."

"We haven't exactly done much training for the coming season yet, have we?" commented Matt.

"Well, we haven't done any recognisable *rugby* training! I can't speak for you, but I feel a heck of a lot fitter than at the start of the holiday."

"It's definitely an added bonus to all this. Do you realise, we stayed in the different time periods for a month, in both of our adventures, and it's still only the second week of the summer holidays?"

"Which means that we have four weeks left; and that means that we can have at least four more adventures this summer!" James concluded, happily.

"What do you think happens to the real characters we seem to be whilst we are in these places, James?"

"To be honest I haven't a clue, but I'm forming ideas. When I am a little more convinced, I'll tell you."

Matt nodded and stood up. He sighed and began to edge along the ridge, disappearing behind the falling water, followed closely by James.

Once inside the cave, James asked Matt if he thought they'd ever return.

"You asked me that last time!"

"Did I?"

"Yes! The answer is, I don't know, James, my old mate!" said Matt, clapping his friend on the shoulder. "But one thing's for sure, our next adventure lies somewhere out there!" He pointed back towards the waterfall.

"Yeah, but shall we go home and get some sleep, first?"

"Good idea, and then I'm planning to research our friend John Ryan to discover what happened to him after we left."

"We could do that with Marty and Pete too." "Another good idea, my friend!

The Walking With Series
by
C. S. CLIFFORD

Walking with the Hood
ISBN: 9 780993 195730

Walking with Nessie
ISBN: 9 780993 195709

Walking with the Fishermen
ISBN: 9 780993 195723

Walking with the Magician
ISBN: 9 780993 195778

Walking with Big Foot
ISBN: 9 780993 195792

Walking with the Smugglers
ISBN: 9 780993 195716

Walking with Mermaids
ISBN: 9 781999 361136

Walking with the Dambusters
ISBN: 9 781999 361150

C. S. Clifford has always been passionate about stories and storytelling. As a child he earned money singing at weddings in the church choir; the proceeds of which were spent in the local bookshop.

As a former primary teacher, he was inspired to start writing through the constant requests of the children he taught. He lives in Kent where, when not writing or promoting and teaching writing, he enjoys carpentry, sea and freshwater angling and exploring the history of his local countryside